Spotting
BIRDS

IN BRITAIN AND EUROPE

Spotting
BIRDS

IN BRITAIN AND EUROPE

An illustrated guide to the top 100 birds

DAVID ALDERTON

LORENZ BOOKS

This edition is published by Lorenz Books

Lorenz Books is an imprint of
Anness Publishing Ltd
Hermes House
88–89 Blackfriars Road
London SE1 8HA
tel. 020 7401 2077; fax 020 7633 9499
www.lorenzbooks.com; info@anness.com

© Anness Publishing Ltd 2004

UK agent: The Manning Partnership Ltd
6 The Old Dairy, Melcombe Road
Bath BA2 3LR
tel. 01225 478444; fax 01225 478440
sales@manning-partnership.co.uk

UK distributor: Grantham Book Services Ltd
Isaac Newton Way
Alma Park Industrial Estate
Grantham
Lincs NG31 9SD
tel. 01476 541080; fax 01476 541061
orders@gbs.tbs-ltd.co.uk

North American agent/distributor: National Book Network
4501 Forbes Boulevard
Suite 200, Lanham, MD 20706
tel. 301 459 3366; fax 301 429 5746
www.nbnbooks.com

Australian agent/distributor: Pan Macmillan Australia
Level 18, St Martins Tower
31 Market St, Sydney, NSW 2000
tel. 1300 135 113; fax 1300 135 103
customer.service@macmillan.com.au

New Zealand agent/distributor: David Bateman Ltd
30 Tarndale Grove, Off Bush Road
Albany, Auckland
tel. (09) 415 7664; fax (09) 415 8892

A CIP catalogue record for this book is available from the British Library.

Publisher: Joanna Lorenz
Editorial Director: Helen Sudell
Project Editor: Ann Kay
Copy Editor/Additional text: Molly Perham
Editorial Reader: Penelope Goodare
Illustrators: Cy Baker/Wildlife Art, Peter Barrett, Anna Childs, Anthony Duke (location
maps), Studio Galante, Martin Knowelden, Andrew Robinson, Tim Thackeray
Design: Howells Design Ltd
Production Controller: Wanda Burrows

All photographs © Anness Publishing Ltd, except for:
p6 left: © David Tipling/naturepl.com; p13 top left: © Dennis Avon;
p15 bottom left: © Simon King/naturepl.com; p18 bottom right: © Dennis Avon

1 3 5 7 9 10 8 6 4 2

C O N T E N T S

Introduction

Bird-spotting is a popular activity and it can be done in any location. Many people enjoy simply watching the birds that come to their garden, but a greater variety can be seen by going out into the countryside or visiting the seashore.

◀ This bird feeder has perching bars and is filled with special unsalted peanuts that are safe for birds. A bird table or feeder should be high off the ground, away from cats.

▲ A pair of binoculars is always very useful for bird-spotting trips. Keep them hanging round your neck, ready for use the minute you spot a bird.

Whether you live in a town or in the countryside, you will be able to spot a number of different birds and learn to identify them. Encourage birds into the garden by putting out scraps of food such as cheese, breadcrumbs, slices of left-over baked potato, or left-over cooked rice and pasta. Providing a bird table helps to protect the birds from cats – making your own table is great fun and much easier than you might think. A small bird bath or bowl will also be welcome. Even if you have no garden, a bird feeder hung outside a window attracts birds such as sparrows, tits and finches. Or simply scatter food on a windowsill.

You will be able to see a greater variety of birds in your local park or wood (make sure you are with an adult when you are out and about). For bird-watching you need a sharp eye and a keen ear for distinguishing their song. A pair of binoculars is useful, and a copy of this book for identifying birds. Carry a small notepad if possible, to jot down any birds you spot, and what they are doing (carrying nesting material, for example). If you visit the same place regularly, you will be able to observe each bird's pattern of behaviour throughout the year. You will also see different species (kinds) of bird depending on the time of year.

Looking for birds

Before long, you will get to know all the common birds in your garden and local area. To find new species of birds you will need to explore farther afield, in open countryside, beside rivers and lakes, in marshland, or on the seashore. If you go to the seaside in the spring or autumn, you will be able to watch migration – birds leaving the country to go to a warmer climate or arriving from a place that is colder.

▲ *Blue tits are active, lively birds that are a lot of fun to watch. They are regular visitors to gardens and will happily use any bird tables and nesting boxes that are supplied for them.*

◀ *There are many ways to tempt birds into your garden so you can have fun watching them. Try hanging food treats on the branch of a tree or bush.*

How this book works

In the All About Birds chapter that begins this book, you will discover exactly what kind of creature birds are, and how they mate, rear their young, feed and hunt, as well as ideas for ways in which you can help to protect the world's many wonderful birds. After this come the entries for the 100 birds chosen for this book. These are divided into chapters based on habitat: sea and shore; rivers, lakes and marshes; woodland; open countryside; city and garden. Each bird entry gives a description and illustration, together with pointers to help you identify it. For each bird there is also a fact file, with a map showing its area of distribution, and notes on its distribution, size, habitat, nest, eggs and food. Birdwatch boxes give hints and tips on identifying particular species.

All About Birds

Birds evolved from the reptiles that lived many millions of years ago. Gradually, some of the reptiles lost their teeth and began to grow feathered wings and tails. Nobody knows for certain how birds began to fly. Some scientists think that they climbed on to perches and glided off from there. Others say that they first took off by running fast on two legs in open desert country. Over the centuries thousands of different types of birds have developed, with every imaginable kind of shape and colouring. These different birds have found their own special ways to survive in all kinds of places, right around the world.

What is a Bird?

Birds are the only animals with feathers, but they do belong to the animal kingdom. This kingdom is divided into several different classes, and birds form one class. The two classes nearest to birds are mammals and reptiles – the first birds developed from early reptiles.

Where do birds come from? Scientists think they evolved from two-legged theropods such as *Compsognathus*, a small dinosaur with long arms but no wings and almost certainly no feathers. Since the 1860s, various fossils of a strange bird-like creature have been found. These show teeth, finger claws, feathered wings and the long, bony tail of a reptile. As the oldest known bird, this became known as *Archaeopteryx*, meaning "ancient wings".

Birds are like mammals in having warm blood and backbones, but instead of front legs they have wings, which are very different from those of flying mammals such as bats. In general, birds are more like reptiles than mammals because they lay eggs, and their feathers have developed from the scales that reptiles have.

◀ *Archaeopteryx may have looked like this, but we cannot be sure what colour it was.*

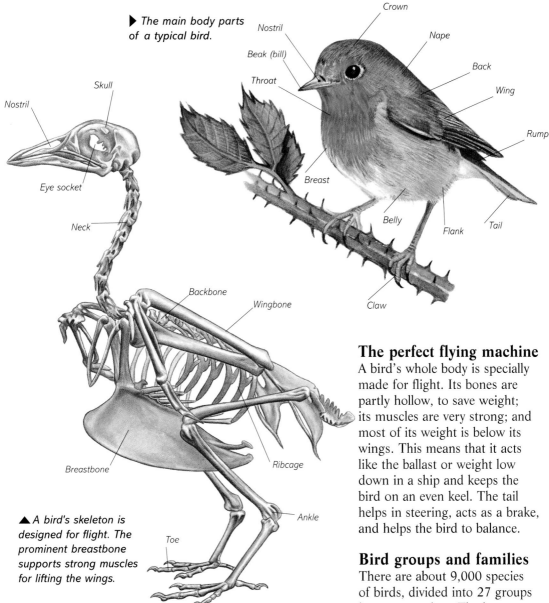

▶ *The main body parts of a typical bird.*

Crown

Nostril

Beak (bill)

Throat

Nostril

Skull

Eye socket

Neck

Nape

Back

Wing

Rump

Breast

Belly

Flank

Tail

Claw

Backbone

Wingbone

Breastbone

Ribcage

Ankle

Toe

▲ *A bird's skeleton is designed for flight. The prominent breastbone supports strong muscles for lifting the wings.*

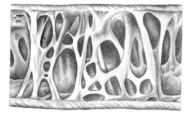

◀ *This shows what some bird bones look like inside. They are hollow but have little bony supports that strengthen them. The skeletons of flying birds need to be very light, to save on the amount of weight carried in the air.*

The perfect flying machine

A bird's whole body is specially made for flight. Its bones are partly hollow, to save weight; its muscles are very strong; and most of its weight is below its wings. This means that it acts like the ballast or weight low down in a ship and keeps the bird on an even keel. The tail helps in steering, acts as a brake, and helps the bird to balance.

Bird groups and families

There are about 9,000 species of birds, divided into 27 groups known as orders. The largest order contains the perching birds and includes more than 5,000 different species. Each order is divided into smaller groups called families. Species in the same family have a similar body shape, making them suited to a particular way of life.

9

Feathers

All birds have feathers, which are important for flight. The fluffy down feathers close to the skin and the contour feathers provide a barrier that keeps warm air close to the bird's body. This helps to maintain the bird's body temperature.

Feathers are made of a tough, flexible substance called keratin. This is also found in human hair and nails. Constant care is needed to keep feathers in good condition. A special oil is produced by the preen gland at the base of the tail. This oil, which is spread over the feathers as the bird preens itself, makes the plumage waterproof. Birds also use their beak like a comb to draw the barbs and barbules together, and also to remove lice and other parasites.

◄ *Kingfishers have particularly colourful plumage (feathers). Both male and female kingfishers are vividly coloured, whereas the male birds of many species are brighter than the females. This helps them to attract female mates.*

TYPES OF FEATHER

Birds have three kinds of feathers. Contour feathers cover the bird's body. Fluffy down feathers lie next to the skin. Flight feathers on the wings are used for flying, while those on the tail help with steering and braking.

Down feather

Flight feather

Contour feather

Shaft

Barbule

Barb

▲ *A flight feather has barbs attached to the shaft. The barbs branch off into smaller barbules.*

◄ *Study a flight feather under a magnifying glass. Split the feather's barbs (individual strands). You can now see the barbules (the fringed edges).*

Legs and Feet

A bird's legs and feet are suited to its particular lifestyle and habitat. Most birds move around by flying, but some spend more time on the ground, or in water. They rely on their running or swimming ability to escape predators and find food.

▲ *Study any bird footprints very carefully. What do they tell you about the bird?*

Many birds have four toes on each foot, arranged to suit the bird's way of life. Birds that perch for much of the time have three toes pointing forwards and one pointing backwards. This allows them to grasp twigs and branches firmly. Woodpeckers have two forward toes and two backward ones – ideal for gripping the bark of trees.

From waders to hunters

Birds that spend much of their time on the water – such as ducks and geese – have webbed feet. The toes are joined by folds of skin so that their feet act as paddles as they swim. Water birds that spend their time standing in water rather than swimming, such as herons, have long legs. Wading birds have long toes, so they can walk over mud.

Birds of prey have long, curved talons for seizing prey. For example, the talons of the golden eagle are so strong that it can lift young lambs into the air.

TYPES OF FEET

Different birds have feet of varied shapes and sizes. When you are trying to identify a bird, look at its legs and feet and ask yourself what kind of habitat or lifestyle they seem best suited to. Hunting? Walking over mud or sand? Paddling in the water?

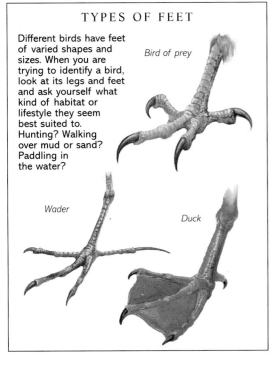

Bird of prey

Wader

Duck

▼ *Long toes can be spread out to make it easier for waders to walk over muddy ground or water plants.*

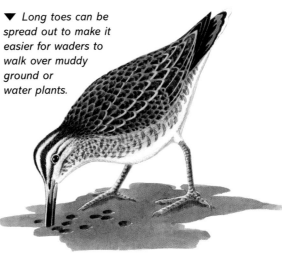

11

How Birds Fly

Some birds, such as swifts, spend much of their lives in the air, whereas others will fly only as a last resort if they are threatened. Different species of birds have different ways of flying, which can help a bird-spotter to identify them in the air.

▲ *The straight, regular flight of ducks such as this mallard is very distinctive. The way in which a bird flies is one of the things that can help you to identify it when you are out bird-spotting.*

Birds are able to fly because their wings produce lift as air currents pass over and under them. The faster the air moves along a surface, the less the air pressure on it. The wing of a bird is rounded on top so that air currents flowing over it have to travel farther and faster than the air moving across the bottom of the wing. The pressure below the wing is greater, and the air currents move upwards towards the lower pressure region above the wing. The wing rises and keeps the bird aloft.

Some birds fly straight with regular wingbeats – ducks and some waders, for example. Others, such as woodpeckers and finches, rise and dip and rise again. Swallows and swifts always seem to be changing direction, while the large soaring birds glide along in an effortless manner.

WING SHAPE AND FLIGHT

A bird's wing is shaped rather like the wing of an aircraft. Both kinds of wing use the same basic principle in order to fly. They are both curved on top and flatter underneath. This shape is called an aerofoil. The curved shape creates low pressure above the wing that allows the bird or aircraft to rise.

Upward lift

Low pressure

▲ *A bird's wing is rounded on top.*

▲ *Section through an aircraft wing.*

High pressure

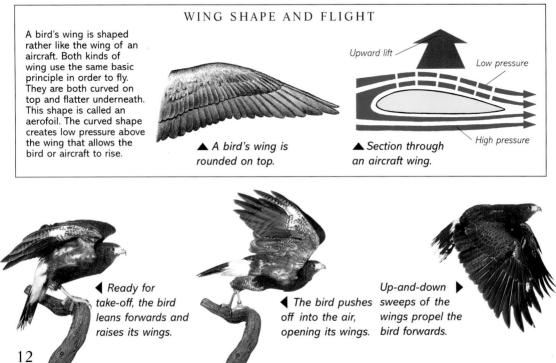

◀ *Ready for take-off, the bird leans forwards and raises its wings.*

◀ *The bird pushes off into the air, opening its wings.*

Up-and-down ▶ sweeps of the wings propel the bird forwards.

Bird Senses

A bird's senses are vital to its survival. They help it to find food, escape from enemies and find mates in the breeding season. Sight is the most important sense for most birds, but some birds rely on other senses to thrive in particular habitats.

▲ *Bird calls are a very important way for birds to communicate with each other, so birds tend to have extremely good hearing.*

All birds' senses are adapted to their environment. The shape of their body reflects which senses are most significant to them, as explained below.

How a bird's senses work

The importance of sight is reflected by the size of the eyes. Birds of prey have large eyes in proportion to their head, and have very keen eyesight. Hearing is very important because birds need to call to each other for all kinds of reasons – to warn of danger, to attract a mate, to establish territory, or to identify their young. Hearing is especially vital for nocturnal birds such as owls, which hunt for food at night.

Some birds have a much more developed sense of touch than others. Snipe have sensitive nerve endings (called corpuscles) in their bills and legs that detect prey and may warn of approaching danger. Few birds have a sense of smell, and most have a relatively small number of taste buds in their mouth.

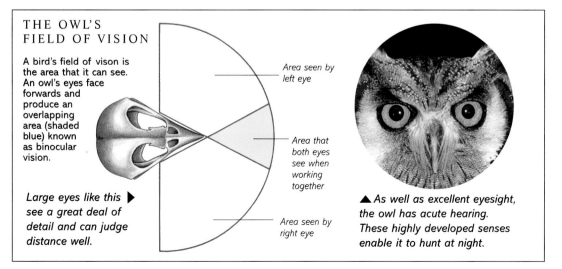

THE OWL'S FIELD OF VISION

A bird's field of vison is the area that it can see. An owl's eyes face forwards and produce an overlapping area (shaded blue) known as binocular vision.

Large eyes like this ▶ see a great deal of detail and can judge distance well.

Area seen by left eye

Area that both eyes see when working together

Area seen by right eye

▲ *As well as excellent eyesight, the owl has acute hearing. These highly developed senses enable it to hunt at night.*

Courtship and Nesting

Each year when spring arrives, birds start to look for a mate. There are species that pair up for just one breeding season, and species that pair for life. Nesting habits also vary. Some birds build elaborate nests, while others make do with a scraped-out hollow on the ground.

▲ *Mute swans are famous for the fact that the same pair stay together for life.*

In spring, the dawn chorus of birdsong means that the breeding season has arrived. A male bird sings or calls to attract a female, and to warn that he has established a territory. He chases away other males of his own species, but allows a female to remain. He then courts her in various ways – singing and dancing or displaying colourful plumage.

Nest-building

When a pair of birds have mated, the building or finding of a nest begins. Each species nests in its own way. The chaffinch, like many small birds, builds a deep, cup-shaped nest hidden from predators high up in leafy branches. Large birds such as rooks and herons build big untidy nests of twigs and sticks that are used again the following spring. Wading and game birds, and ducks and geese, nest on the ground. Water birds such as grebes are not adapted to life on land. Their nests are built on floating platforms.

The stork ▶ builds a nest from twigs. It often nests on rooftops.

◀ *The thrush's nest is made of grass and twigs. To make a hollow for the eggs to sit in, the female bird turns round and round in the centre of the nest.*

Rearing Young

All birds reproduce by laying eggs. The number of eggs laid at a time, known as the clutch, varies between species. The size, shape and colour of birds' eggs also varies, as does the length of time it takes for them to hatch.

Birds sit on their eggs to keep them warm so that the chicks can develop inside the shell. This "incubation" period varies from 10 days to several months. Usually it is the female that sits on the eggs. When a chick is ready to hatch, it makes holes at the blunt end of the shell with its beak, then pushes the top off and emerges. Some chicks can feed themselves very soon after hatching. Others need to be fed and looked after by their parents for some time.

Leaving home

Young birds usually leave the nest 12–30 days after hatching. Many cannot fly at first, as their flight feathers are underdeveloped and their wing muscles are weak. They rest on the sides of the nest, flapping their wings in order to strengthen them. The chicks of game birds (such as pheasants), waterbirds and waders leave the nest soon after hatching. This gives them a better chance of escaping predators.

▲ *Eggs are a good way of identifying birds, but you should never touch or disturb nests and eggs.*

◀ *A mute swan guards her newly hatched chicks.*

Young chicks ready ▶ *for meal time. Keeping chicks fed can be a very time-consuming business. The young of some kinds of bird are fed by their parents as often as 60 times an hour.*

Searching for Food

You can identify a bird by its beak, or bill, almost as often as you can recognize it by its plumage. The shape of a bird's beak can often tell you what kind of food it eats. Different birds eat different kinds of food, and they catch it in different ways.

TYPES OF BEAK

The shape of a bird's beak will tell you what kinds of things a particular type of bird likes to eat.

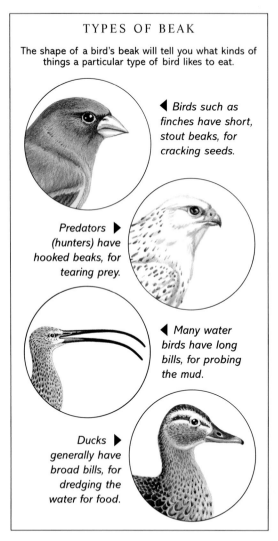

◀ *Birds such as finches have short, stout beaks, for cracking seeds.*

Predators ▶ *(hunters) have hooked beaks, for tearing prey.*

◀ *Many water birds have long bills, for probing the mud.*

Ducks ▶ *generally have broad bills, for dredging the water for food.*

M any birds depend on plants for their food, eating fruit, seeds, nuts, flowers and other plant matter. Their diet throughout the year depends on what is available. Certain finches, for example, eat the buds in apple orchards in spring, while later in the year they consume seeds and fruit. A typical finch bill is small and stout, which helps these birds to crack seeds easily. Some birds collect plant food when it is plentiful to see them through the winter. Jays, for example, store acorns and other seeds.

There are also birds that have a varied diet of insects and worms as well as taking berries and food scraps from the bird table. If you look carefully at the more common garden birds – robins, blackbirds and thrushes, for example – you will see that they have a "general purpose" beak that is suitable for several different kinds of food.

Around the base of trees is a good place to ▶ *look for remains that might tell you which bird has been feeding in the area. If you find an owl's pellet, for example, soak it in water so that it falls apart. You will then be able to see exactly what the owl has been eating.*

Water-feeders

Birds that take food from water have other kinds of bill. Ducks have a broad bill for dredging food on or just below the water's surface. Divers, such as the great crested grebe, have straight, spear-shaped bills. Waders such as the curlew have a long, curved bill to probe mud, while the heron's beak is long and straight, for stabbing prey. Birds that skim across the water, such as the Sandwich tern, have the lower part of their beaks longer than the upper part, so they can scoop up prey while on the wing.

Hunters and scavengers

Most birds of prey catch prey with their talons and then use their strong, hooked beaks for tearing the flesh apart. Some, such as the sparrowhawk, mostly eat other birds. Others catch small mammals, often swallowing them whole. The bones and fur are hard to digest, so owls cough them up in pellets – little packets of bones wrapped in fur. When food is scarce, many predators scavenge for food, feeding on carcasses of dead lambs, say, or on animals killed on the road. Vultures are well-known scavengers, often seen foraging on garbage tips.

◀ Nut shells that have been gnawed by animals can be a good sign of birds to be found nearby. Squirrels and mice leave teeth marks and neat holes. Birds leave jagged edges or peck-marks or crack nuts in two, like the top two nuts here.

Many birds ▶ like fruit. Look for large, uneven-sized holes – these are often left by garden birds such as thrushes and blackbirds.

MAKE A BIRD-CAKE

1. Feed birds yourself with this tasty bird-cake. Soften some lard or fat on a radiator or get an adult to help you melt it in a saucepan. Mix the fat with chopped nuts, oatmeal and cake or bread crumbs.

2. Cut a long piece of string. Tie a really large knot in one end of the string. Put the string into a plastic cup so that the knotted end is at the bottom. Now spoon your fatty mixture into the cup.

3. Wait until the mixture is completely set and cold. Pull the string gently to remove the cake. Hang it from a tree or bush branch and notice which kinds of birds eat it.

Camouflage

The way in which birds and other creatures disguise themselves is called camouflage. It is usually to enable them to surprise prey or to hide from predators. Some birds blend into the surrounding vegetation, while others look like pebbles or shingle on the beach.

▲ *The white feathers of the snowy owl make it almost invisible against the snowy landscape of its natural home habitat.*

Birds are very vulnerable to predators and their chances of survival are greater if they cannot be easily seen. Species that spend much of their time on the wing are generally lighter in colour underneath than above, so that enemies from below cannot spot them so readily against the sky. Other birds have plumage that matches their usual habitat, so that they can blend into the background.

Protecting their young

The females of ground-nesting birds, such as pheasants and mallard ducks, are less brightly coloured than the males. This duller plumage helps to camouflage females when sitting on the nest. The female ringed plover lays spotted eggs that blend in with the nest, which is a gravel scrape on the ground. Her black, white and brown banded markings break up her outline so she is well hidden from predators when sitting on the eggs. If both parents of a ground-nesting species sit on the nest, then both will have similar, suitable coloration.

▼ *The nightjar's greyish-brown mottled plumage provides good camouflage when it rests on the ground.*

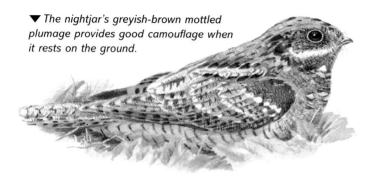

The colouring of the ringed plover ▶ *blends in with the lake shores and gravel beds where it is often found.*

Migration

Some birds live in the same place all year round, but others are only temporary visitors.
The availability of food, the search for a suitable nest and seasonal changes in weather
are the main reasons why birds migrate.

▲ *The Arctic tern migrates farther than any other bird. In the course of one year, it flies from the Arctic to the Antarctic and back again.*

Great flocks of birds gathering for their winter migration are a common sight each autumn. How they find their way to and from their destination is one of nature's wonders. Many birds migrate in a large flock, so adult birds can teach young birds on their first migration where to go. However, some birds, such as the cuckoo, set out on their own and reach their destination without being shown the way. Experiments have shown that birds navigate using the Earth's magnetic field and the position of the sun and stars, and also by following familiar landmarks.

Well suited to travel

The swallow is a famous migrant. Its arrival in Europe from southern Africa marks the start of summer. By the time it leaves in the autumn, it may have raised two or three broods. Like its relative, the house martin, the swallow is well suited to long-distance flight, with its slim, streamlined body and curved, narrow wings. Large migratory birds, such as the white stork, use thermals (rising columns of air) on their journey, soaring upwards on one thermal and then gliding down towards another.

This map shows some of the greatest ▶
bird journeys (see key below).

■ *Peregrine falcons migrate from Canada all the way to Argentina.*

▨ *Swallows migrate from northern Europe and Asia to South Africa and back again – nearly 20,000 km/12,400 miles.*

■ *Arctic Tern (see caption above).*

■ *White storks travel from Europe to South Africa via Gibraltar or the Middle East.*

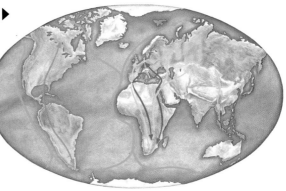

Watching Birds

Birds can be seen in almost any locality, even in the centre of cities. You don't need any equipment to watch birds, but a pair of binoculars will allow you to study birds in more detail. The scientific name for the study of birds is ornithology.

▲ *Always try to jot down at least a few notes there and then. It is always difficult to remember things once you are back home again.*

There are three rules to bird-spotting. First, be patient. Birds are busy with their own lives and will not appear just when you want them to. The second rule is to be very still and quiet. Birds are often shy, with keen eyesight and hearing. They are always on the watch for enemies, so you will not see or hear many birds if you crash about or chatter to friends. The third rule is never go bird-watching on your own, and always tell an adult where you are going. Also, do not get into dangerous situations such as wading into deep water, climbing trees or peering over steep cliff-edges when looking for birds.

Starting out

You cannot expect, if you are a beginner, to identify every bird the first time you see it. It is a good idea to take a notebook and pencil with you, so you can write down details of the birds that you see and draw sketches of them. The things you might want to note down are:

- size and shape
- colour and markings
- how the bird moves
- call notes or song
- habitat
- date and time

You could do a simple ▶ sketch when the bird is in front of you and make notes about coloration, then colour in the picture at home.

BIRD-WATCHING EQUIPMENT

Here are some items that you may find useful when you are out bird-spotting.

Binoculars

Roll-up mat

Suitable footwear

Notebook, pen, pencils and perhaps crayons

Size, shape and markings

Compare the bird's general size and shape with a common bird that you know well. Note down the size and shape of the bill, legs, wings, tail and neck. What is the general colour of the bird, on top and underneath? Does it have any marks or patches, and what colour are they? What colour are the bill, legs, feet and eyes?

How the bird moves

If the bird is in the air, does it fly directly like a crow, or have a bounding flight like a finch? Does it hover like a kestrel, or plummet-dive, like a tern? If the bird is on the ground, does it run like a starling or hop like a blackbird?

Call notes or song

Birds can often be heard but not seen, so get to know the call notes of different birds.

Habitat

Where did you see the bird – in woodland, open country, beside a pond or river? Birds usually remain in their own particular habitat.

Date and time

Note down the date and time when you see a bird, and what it is doing. Activity in the breeding season is especially interesting, when birds are nesting and raising young.

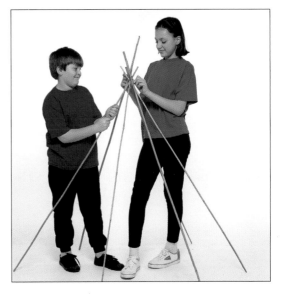

◀ ▲ *A "hide" is a shelter from which you can watch birds. Make a simple teepee-style hide from garden canes tied together with string and a tarpaulin fixed on with safety pins, and perhaps tent pegs. Camouflage your hide with leaves and twigs.*

DRAWING BIRDS

Before you start to draw, study the bird closely. What is the size and shape of the bill, legs, wings, tail and neck? Drawing birds is actually fairly easy if you work in simple stages.

1. With a pencil, draw an egg shape for the body and a smaller egg for the head. Add circles and lines to position and sketch the other parts.

2. Now use a black felt-tip pen to ink in the shape of the bird. Be careful not to ink in any unwanted pencil planning lines.

3. Erase any unwanted pencil lines. Use coloured pencils, crayons or paints to colour your bird and add in more detail.

Conservation

It has been estimated that three-quarters of the world's birds may come under threat in the twenty-first century. By banning hunting, protecting habitats, setting up reserves and reducing pollution many birds could be saved.

When woodland is cut down to make way for a housing estate, or meadows are ploughed up to grow crops, many birds lose their natural habitats. Others are increasingly threatened by the pollution of lakes and rivers. In agricultural areas, chemicals that are sprayed on the fields to kill weeds and pests also kill the food that birds rely on. Over-fishing depletes fish stocks and reduces the amount of fish available for seabirds. There are many different threats to birds' survival, most of them caused by human activity. However, more and more people are becoming aware of these problems and realizing the need for conservation.

▲ *Seabirds such as puffins are becoming much rarer in some places because the fish that provide their main food are disappearing. In British waters, puffin numbers have fallen dramatically around Shetland since the 1970s for this reason.*

Oil pollution

Each year thousands of birds are found dead around our coasts as a result of oil spills. Migrating species are particularly at risk when they look for areas of calm water on which to rest or fish. Oil-covered seas look calm, but if a bird alights in the middle of a slick, it soon becomes covered and unable to fly away, or it may be poisoned by contact with the oil.

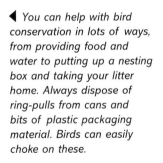

You can help with bird conservation in lots of ways, from providing food and water to putting up a nesting box and taking your litter home. Always dispose of ring-pulls from cans and bits of plastic packaging material. Birds can easily choke on these.

Hang your bird table from a strong tree branch in your garden.

Conservation groups

Rescuing birds from oil spills is just one of the jobs done by bird conservation groups. They campaign against pollution, help to preserve natural habitats and set up bird reserves. They also breed endangered species and reintroduce them into the wild. Find out if there are any bird reserves or conservation groups in your area by asking at your school or library.

How else can you help?

Providing food for birds in winter is helpful. Once you begin feeding, you must continue through the year, as the birds will come to depend on you. Food should be in hanging feeders or on a bird table, where birds are safe from cats and the food will not attract rats. Some nuts and seeds are sold specially for wild birds, and many kitchen scraps are suitable. Avoid uncooked dried beans and rice, and salty items such as salted nuts. Also, avoid peanuts in spring, as young birds can choke on these. You should also provide fresh water, especially when other supplies are frozen.

Play a part in bird conservation by putting out food on a bird table. Get an adult to help you make your own table from a large plywood board with narrow strips of wood glued around the edge. Screw eye-hooks into each corner and attach some strings.

Bird Habitats

A bird's "habitat" is its natural home, where it is suited to live. When bird-spotting, it helps to know which birds to expect in which habitat. The five main kinds of European habitat are shown below, and the birds that belong in each kind are described in the chapters that follow.

Sea and shore

The ocean provides a rich source of food for seabirds. Fish, molluscs, plankton and marine invertebrates such as krill form the basis of their diet. Many seabirds are social creatures by nature, nesting in huge colonies. These colonies may be on rocky outcrops by the sea, on islands off the coast, or on the shore. Both the eggs and chicks of species of bird that breed on the shore have markings that mean they are very effectively camouflaged among the sand or pebbles, keeping them safe from predators.

Rivers, lakes and marshes

In freshwater habitats, the speed at which the water flows determines the kind of vegetation that grows there. This in turn influences the types of birds that are found in that spot. However, it is not all about food. Some kinds of birds are certainly drawn to rivers, lakes and marshes mainly for food. Others, however, may seek sheltered nesting sites and safety from predators in among the reedbeds.

Woodland

Deciduous woods provide all kinds of bird-food. The actual trees supply acorns, seeds and nuts. The rich leaf "litter" found at the base of trees is full of insect larvae, slugs, centipedes and woodlice. Fewer bird species are found in coniferous forests as the food is less varied, although owls eat small mammals such as voles that live there.

Open countryside

This includes several types of habitat. Heathland and moors attract birds of prey such as the hen harrier, as well as ground-nesting birds such as the nightjar. In farmland, hedges used to provide food and shelter for birds, while farm buildings offered nest sites to pigeons, swallows and house martins. Modern farming practices, however, have forced many birds to find new homes.

City and garden

A city's concrete, cars and crowds might seem to hold little appeal to wildlife, yet many birds thrive there. Cities include a variety of habitats. The centre may contain tall, cliff-like buildings in its industrial areas or patches of wasteland, where doves and pigeons set up home. Leafy suburbs filled with parks and gardens are loved by birds such as blackbirds and tits.

25

Sea and Shore

Some seabirds, such as terns, live largely on the wing, hovering over the water before diving in search of fish. Their long, pointed wings are an indication of their aerial ability. Other seabirds, such as the little auk, have a more aquatic lifestyle. The auks have sometimes been described as "penguins of the north". Waders inhabit shallow waters along the shore. They are often seen in mixed groups, walking along a beach at low tide or searching for food in the mudflats. Gulls are a familiar sight at the seaside, but some species have spread inland to live alongside people.

Puffin

Fratercula arctica

These members of the auk family have brightly coloured bills that resemble those of parrots. Young puffins have much narrower and less colourful bills than the adults. When underwater, puffins use their wings like flippers, enabling them to swim faster. Puffins come ashore to nest in colonies on cliffs and in coastal areas, where they can breed largely hidden from predators. Sand eels form an important part of their diet at this time, and adult birds often fly long distances to find food. Adult birds fly back to their young with eels arranged in a row, hanging down each side of their bill. They can carry as many as ten at a time in this way.

▲ *The puffin's bill varies depending on the bird's age and the time of year.*

IDENTIFICATION

- Whitish sides to the face, with black extending back over the crown. Sides of the face greyish during the winter.

- Black neck, back and wings; underparts white, with a grey area on the flanks.

- Broad, flattened bill with red area running down its length and across the tip.

- Sexes are alike.

▼ *Puffins make nesting tunnels underground or use existing holes.*

FACT FILE

Distribution Throughout the northern Atlantic, including Spitzbergen

Size 32cm/13in

Habitat Sea and coastal areas

Nest Underground burrows

Eggs 1, white

Food Fish

Little Auk

Alle alle

The little auk has very little neck and a short, stubby body.

Although not widely distributed, little auks may be the world's most numerous seabirds. During the brief summer, huge nesting colonies gather in the Arctic. They then head south as winter approaches and the sea starts to freeze. Little auks are more likely to be spotted at this time of year, flying low over the waves, or even through them. If fierce storms make feeding very difficult, then these birds, in a weakened state, may be driven into coastal areas.

IDENTIFICATION

- In summer, the head and upper chest are black. The back, wings and upper surface of the tail are also black, except for white wing streaks.
- In winter, white appears on the face, leaving a black band across the throat.
- The bill is small and black.
- Sexes are alike.

FACT FILE

Distribution Icelandic coast to northern Scandinavia, across the North Sea to the coast of eastern England
Size 20cm/8in
Habitat: Sea and coastal areas
Nest Cliffs or crevices
Eggs 1, pale blue
Food Microscopic plankton

Great Skua

Catharacta skua

◀ *The great skua is a large, impressive-looking bird.*

These powerful birds can look like buzzards as they soar above the ocean. When landing on the sea, great skuas glide down and hover in an unusual way before finally touching down. They find food as and when they can, catching fish or stealing it from other seabirds. During the breeding period, when they spend time on land, they may eat foods such as berries, or even catch small rodents.

IDENTIFICATION

- Mostly dull brown with lighter streaking and barring. White wing flashes.
- Powerful hooked bill.
- Sexes similar but hens may have more yellowish-brown markings on the neck.

The distinctive white wing flashes are particularly visible when the great skua is in flight.

FACT FILE

Distribution Ranges widely throughout the Atlantic Ocean
Size 50–58cm/20–23in
Habitat Sea and coastal areas
Nest Depression on the ground
Eggs 2, olive grey to reddish brown with darker markings
Food Typically fish and carrion

Herring Gull

Larus argentatus

These large gulls are often seen on fishing jetties and around harbours, searching for scraps. They have also moved inland and can be seen in areas such as rubbish dumps, where they scavenge for food, often in quite large groups. Herring gulls are noisy by nature, especially when breeding. They now frequently nest on rooftops in coastal towns and cities, a trend that began as recently as the 1940s in Britain. Pairs can become very aggressive at breeding time, swooping menacingly on people who venture close to the nest site or even to the chicks once they fledge.

The colour of the herring gull's wings varies from silver grey to slate grey.

The herring gull's pink legs are a distinctive feature.

The black flight feathers have prominent, large white spots.

The head and neck are white, with some dark streaking appearing in winter.

The herring gull has a stouter bill than many other species of gull.

FACT FILE

IDENTIFICATION

- White head and underparts, with grey on the back and wings.
- Prominent large white spots on the black flight feathers.
- Distinctive pink legs and feet.
- Reddish spot towards the tip of the lower bill.
- Some dark streaking on the head and neck during the winter.
- Sexes are alike.
- Young birds are mainly brown, with prominent barring on their wings and dark bills.

BIRDWATCH

The herring gull may be confused with the common gull, due to their similar black and white wing tip feathers. The herring gull is larger, with distinctive flesh-pink legs and a bright red spot on its bill. The common gull has yellow-green legs.

Distribution Atlantic, north of Iceland and south to northern coast of Spain, through the North Sea and Baltic areas, north of Scandinavia

Size 60cm/24in

Habitat Coastal and inland areas

Nest Small pile of vegetation

Eggs 2–3, pale blue to brown with darker markings

Food Fish and carrion

Black-headed Gull

Larus ridibundus

In winter, the bill is red at the base and dark at the tip.

These gulls move inland in winter, to town parks with lakes. They are also often seen following tractors ploughing at this time of year, seeking worms and grubs in the soil. Black-headed gulls nest close to water in quite large colonies. Like many gulls, they are noisy birds, even calling at night. On warm summer evenings, they can be seen chasing flying ants and similar insects in flight, demonstrating their agility in the air.

IDENTIFICATION

- In summer, a distinctive black head with a white collar and white underparts.
- In winter, the head is white with black ear coverts and black smudges over the eyes.
- Grey wings with black flight feathers.

▲ The head is mainly white in the winter. Black feathering on the head appears only in the summer.

FACT FILE

Distribution Across most of Europe into Asia. Also present on the North African side of the Mediterranean

Size 39cm/15in

Habitat Coastal areas

Nest Scrape lined with plant matter

Eggs 2–3, pale blue to brown with darker markings

Food Typically molluscs, various crustaceans and small fish

Great Black-backed Gull

Larus marinus

The lower bill has a red area at its tip.

These large gulls can be very disruptive when close to nesting seabird colonies. They harry other birds for their catches of fish, and also take eggs and chicks. In winter, they move inland to scavenge on rubbish tips. Many great black-backed gulls overwinter in Britain, returning in spring to breed in Norway. Pairs are often solitary at this time, especially if nesting near people, but they are more likely to nest in colonies on uninhabited islands.

IDENTIFICATION

- White head and underparts with black on the back and wings. White spots on black tail and large white area at wing tips.
- Yellow bill with red tip to lower bill.
- Pale pinkish legs.
- Sexes are alike.

The large area of white at the wing tips is seen especially clearly in flight.

FACT FILE

Distribution From northern Spain north to Iceland and eastwards through the North Sea and Baltic to Scandinavia. Also present on the eastern side of North America

Size 74cm/29in

Habitat Coastal areas

Nest Pile of vegetation

Eggs 2–3, brownish with dark markings

Food Fish and carrion

Common Gull

Larus canus

These birds range over a wide area inland, seeking earthworms and other invertebrates to eat. In sandy coastal regions they also hunt for shellfish. They leave their breeding grounds in Scandinavia and Russia at the end of summer and head south to France and the Mediterranean, where they overwinter before migrating north again in spring. Common gulls bully smaller gulls such as the black-headed gull and take their food. Both species are found in the same kind of inland areas: grassland and agricultural land.

Distribution Iceland, Great Britain and the Baltic region. Main breeding grounds are in Scandinavia and Russia. Extends across Asia to western North America

Size 46cm/18in

Habitat Coasts and inland areas that are close to water

Nest Raised nest of twigs and other debris

Eggs 2–3, pale blue to brownish olive with dark markings

Food Shellfish, small fish and invertebrates

IDENTIFICATION

- White head and underparts. Greyish wings with white markings at the tips. Black flight feathers with white spots. White tail. Yellow bill and yellow-green legs.

- In winter, greyish streaking on the head.

- Sexes are alike.

- Young birds have brown mottled plumage.

The legs are yellow-green.

Gannet

Northern gannet *Sula bassana*

Pale yellow plumage extends down the neck.

This species is the largest of all gannets and can weigh up to 3.6kg/8lb. The gannets' keen eyesight allows them to detect shoals of fish such as herring and mackerel in the ocean below. When feeding, they dive down into a shoal and seize fish from under the water. Their streamlined shape also enables them to swim. Breeding takes place in the spring, when they form large squabbling colonies. The young mature slowly and are unlikely to breed until they are at least four years old.

Distribution Along the eastern seaboard of North America extending across the Atlantic via southern Greenland and Iceland beyond Norway, southwards through the Mediterranean and down to the west coast of North Africa

Size 88–100cm/ 35–39in

Habitat Sea

Nest Usually on cliffs, built from seaweed and other marine debris held together by droppings

Eggs 1, whitish

Food Fish

IDENTIFICATION

- Mainly white. Yellow on head and neck and black flight feathers. Feet are dark grey.

- Sexes are alike.

- Young birds are dark brown in colour.

Common Tern

Sterna hirundo

Common terns are found in the colder parts of their range, in Scandinavia and northern Europe, between April and October. In the autumn they head south to warmer places in southern and western Africa, where they overwinter. Travelling long distances means that they have to be powerful flyers, but they are also very agile. Their strong forked tails help them to hover and adjust position before diving in search of fish. They have long bills to catch fish, and this distinguishes them from gulls. Common terns are very versatile in their feeding habits. They may hunt for food on the wing or dive into the oceans to obtain their quarry.

A distinctive black cap on the top of the head extends down the face to include the eye area and also down the back of the neck.

The long red bill turns black in winter.

The common tern has a long body shape.

The flight feathers are long, and there are narrow white streamers on the tail.

The legs and feet are red, and the legs are very short, but longer than those of the Arctic tern.

FACT FILE

IDENTIFICATION

- Long body shape with black on the top of the head extending down the back of the neck.
- Rest of the face and underparts whitish grey.
- Back and wings greyish, with long flight feathers. Narrow white streamers on the tail.
- Bill red, aside from the dark tip. Bill becomes completely black in the winter.
- The plumage in front of the eyes becomes white during this time.
- Legs and feet red.
- Sexes are alike.

BIRDWATCH

Some colonies of nesting terns contain more than 1,000 birds. Always keep your distance, as the birds are easily disturbed. They may attack, swooping at the head or striking out with beaks and feet. They have been known to draw blood.

Distribution Great Britain and Scandinavia and much of central Europe during the summer, migrating south to parts of western and southern Africa for the winter months

Size 36cm/14in

Habitat Near water

Nest Scrape on the ground

Eggs 3, pale brown with dark spots

Food Mainly fish, but also eats crustaceans

31

Sandwich Tern

Cabot's tern *Sterna sandvicensis*

A summer visitor to northern Europe, this species is often sighted slightly earlier than the common tern and then leaves just before its relative. The Sandwich tern is significantly larger, and also surprisingly noisy – the sound of its calls has been likened to a grating cartwheel. Although Sandwich terns may skim over the water surface seeking food, they also dive spectacularly from heights of as much as 10m/33ft. They usually breed in high-density colonies in the open on sand bars and similarly exposed coastal sites, although they may sometimes nest on islands in lakes.

The wings of the Sandwich tern are long and narrow.

The tern's forked tail distinguishes it from a gull.

FACT FILE

Distribution Found around the shores of Great Britain and northern Europe, as well as the Caspian and Black seas, wintering further south in the Mediterranean region and Africa. Also found in parts of southern Asia, the Caribbean and South America

Size 43cm/17in

Habitat Coastal areas

Nest Scrape on the ground

Eggs 1–2, brownish white with darker markings

Food Fish, especially sand eels

IDENTIFICATION

- Shaggy black crest evident at the back of the head.

- Entire top of the head is black during the summer, while a white forehead is characteristic of the winter plumage.

- Long black bill with a yellow tip.

- Rest of the head and underparts are white, and the wings are grey.

- Sexes are alike.

BIRDWATCH

It can be difficult to distinguish between a gull and a tern. Gulls are larger and fatter, and their wings are broader and blunter. Terns are more slender and graceful. They have long wings and a deeply forked tail, and a thin, more pointed beak.

Roseate Tern

Sterna dougallii

In northern parts of their range, roseate terns are brief summer visitors, only likely to be present from about the middle of May until the end of August. They are most likely to be seen where the shore is shallow and sandy, providing them with better fishing opportunities. They dive into the water to catch their prey from heights of no more than 2m/7ft. They may also take fish from other terns, and their shorter wings and quicker wing beats make them more agile in flight. Unlike some other terns, roseate terns avoid open areas when nesting, preferring sites that are concealed among rocks or vegetation. They have a distinctive harsh "aach aach" call note.

IDENTIFICATION

- Pinkish tinge on the whitish underparts.
- Relatively long tail streamers and quite short wings.
- Bill primarily blackish with a red base in the summer.
- Entire top of the head black in summer; forehead white in winter.
- Sexes are alike.

FACT FILE

Distribution The British Isles south to Spain and North Africa. Winters in western Africa

Size 36cm/14in

Habitat Coastal areas

Nest Scrape on the ground

Eggs 1–2, cream or buff with reddish-brown markings

Food Mainly fish

Arctic Tern

Sterna paradisaea

It can be very difficult to distinguish this species from the common tern, but the Arctic tern's bill is shorter and does not have a black tip in the summer. The tail is longer, and the tail streamers are very evident in flight. Arctic terns undertake the most extensive migrations of any birds, flying almost from one end of the world to the other. Breeding near the Arctic Circle, they then head south, often beyond Africa to Antarctica, before repeating the journey the following year, although it appears that some young birds stay for their first full year in the Antarctic Ocean. Arctic terns nest communally, often on islands.

IDENTIFICATION

- Black area covering the entire top of the head, with white chest and underparts.
- Wings grey.
- Bill dark red, becoming black in the winter when the forehead is white.
- Sexes are alike.

FACT FILE

Distribution Breeds in northern Europe and the Arctic, overwintering in southern Africa

Size 38cm/15in

Habitat Seas and also fresh water

Nest Hollow on the ground, lined with vegetation

Eggs 2, brownish, bluish or greenish with dark markings

Food Fish and invertebrates

Eurasian Oystercatcher

Haematopus ostralegus

The large size of these waders, coupled with their noisy nature, makes them quite conspicuous. The oystercatcher's powerful bill is a surprisingly adaptable tool, allowing these birds not only to force mussel shells apart, but also to hammer limpets off groynes and even prey on crabs. Inland, oystercatchers use their bills to catch earthworms in the soil. Individuals will defend favoured feeding sites, such as a mussel bed, from others of their own kind, although oystercatchers may sometimes form large flocks of thousands of birds, especially during the winter.

Black feathers cover the upper body, head and upper chest.

The underparts are white.

The Eurasian oystercatcher's long legs turn a pale pink colour in winter.

The powerful bill is ideal for prising shellfish apart.

FACT FILE

IDENTIFICATION

- Black head, back, upper chest and wings.
- White underparts and a white stripe on the wings.
- Prominent, straight orangish-red bill, which may be shorter and thicker in cock birds.
- Legs are reddish.
- In winter plumage, adults have a white throat and collar and pale pink legs.
- Sexes are alike.

BIRDWATCH

Waders can often be identified by their call. The oystercatcher makes a penetrating "kleep" sound, a shorter "pic pic" call, and a loud communal piping display. The stone curlew's call sounds like "curlee", and can be heard up to 2.5km/1.5m away.

Distribution Around the shores of Europe, especially Great Britain, extending to Asia. Also present in North Africa

Size 44cm/17in

Habitat Tidal mudflats, sometimes in fields

Nest Scrape on the ground

Eggs 2–4, light buff with blackish-brown markings

Food Cockles, mussels and similar prey

Stone Curlew

Thick knee *Burhinus oedicnemus*

The stone curlew is a wader that has adapted to a relatively dry environment. Its mottled plumage enables it to blend in well against a stony background. When frightened, it drops to the ground in an attempt to conceal its presence. These birds are often active after dark, when they will be much harder to observe. On occasion, stone curlews living close to coastal areas fly to mudflats, feeding when the flats are exposed by the sea.

The wings have white wing bars edged with black.

IDENTIFICATION

- Streaked neck, upper breast and wings, with clear white stripes above and below eyes. White wing bars with black edges. Abdomen and throat are whitish.
- Bill mainly blackish, but yellow at the base.
- Yellowish legs.
- Sexes are alike.

The stone curlew has long, thick, yellowish legs.

FACT FILE

Distribution Breeds at various different localities across Europe, extending from southern England southwards. Also ranges into southern Asia and south to certain parts of North Africa

Size 45cm/18in

Habitat Open, relatively dry countryside

Nest Bare scrape on the ground

Eggs 2, pale buff with dark markings

Food Invertebrates, typically caught at night

Ringed Plover

Greater ringed plover *Charadrius hiaticula*

In winter, the black areas of plumage are reduced.

These relatively small waders have strong migratory instincts. They breed mainly in the far north, and are most likely to be seen in Europe during May and again from the middle of August for about a month. After that time, they leave European shores on their way south to Africa for the winter. Ringed plovers breed on beaches and on the tundra. They can be seen in large flocks outside the nesting season, often seeking food in tidal areas.

IDENTIFICATION

- Black mask across the forehead and eyes. White patch above the bill and behind the eyes. Underparts white, except for black band across chest. Wings a greyish brown.
- Orange, black-tipped bill (all black in winter).
- Sexes are alike.

The ringed plover has orange-yellow legs.

FACT FILE

Distribution Western Europe and North America, wintering in Africa. Also recorded in parts of Asia

Size 19cm/7.5in

Habitat Coastal areas and tundra

Nest Bare scrape on the ground

Eggs 4, stone-buff with black markings

Food Freshwater and marine invertebrates

35

King Eider

Somateria spectabilis

Like most birds from the far north, the king eider's range extends right around the top of the globe. These sea ducks thrive off the cold northern coasts of Europe, America and Asia, just south of the permanent ice line. King eiders move with the seasons more widely than other species of eider. Huge groups of up to 100,000 birds may congregate together during the moulting period. These groups split up during the breeding season, when pairs nest individually across the Arctic tundra. The females line their nests with breast feathers, which are particularly soft and warm. King eiders are powerful swimmers and dive to obtain their food.

This is the only waterbird to appear black when seen from the back and white when seen from the front.

The drake has a bright orange forehead.

Female eiders have mottled brown colouring.

The chest is a pinkish white colour.

A mature male eider has two distinctive "sails" on his back.

IDENTIFICATION

- When they are in breeding condition, adult drakes (male ducks) have an orange forehead with a black edge and a reddish bill.

- Light-grey plumage extends down the drake's neck.

- Drake has pinkish-white chest with black wings and underparts.

- Outside of the mating season, drakes are a darker brown, with an orangish-yellow bill and white plumage on the back.

- Ducks are mainly a speckled shade of brown. The pale underside of their wings is visible in flight.

BIRDWATCH

Eiders are large, heavily built marine ducks that are rarely seen inland. The drakes (male ducks) are strikingly patterned, and the king eider is especially distinctive – it is the only waterfowl to appear white in front and black behind when seen at a distance. The ducks (females) are a mottled brown in colouring. Eider females are the only waterfowl with a barred breast.

FACT FILE

Distribution From the coast of Iceland eastwards to Scandinavia in winter. Breeds in the Arctic during short summer there. Also found in North America and Asia.

Size 63cm/25in

Habitat Tundra and open sea

Nest Hollow lined with down feathers

Eggs 4–7, olive buff

Food Mainly crustaceans and marine invertebrates

Avocet

Pied avocet *Recurvirostra avosetta*

Avocets locate food by sweeping their long, thin, upward-curving bill from side to side in the water. They most frequently move about by wading, but can also swim well. In some areas they are present in large numbers, nesting close together. Breeding pairs can be very aggressive. When migrating, avocets fly quite low in loose lines. Birds from eastern areas migrate further than those from the west, overwintering in Africa as well as the Mediterranean region.

IDENTIFICATION

- Black on head and nape. Black flight feathers and stripes on wings and shoulders.

- Long, thin black bill curves up at the tip.

- Long, pale blue legs.

- Hens often have shorter bills and a brown tinge to black markings.

Black stripes extend over the shoulder area and around the sides of the wing.

FACT FILE

Distribution Found in north-western Europe, often close to the coast, southern Europe and North Africa. Range also extends into western Asia

Size 46cm/18in

Habitat Lagoons and mudflats

Nest Scrape on the ground lined with vegetation

Eggs 4, pale brown with faint markings

Food Small crustaceans and other invertebrates

Oldsquaw

Long-tailed duck *Clangula hyemalis*

Outside the breeding season, the head is white on top, with black patches at the sides.

These sea ducks often congregate in large numbers. They spend most of their time on the water, and obtain food by diving under the waves. They come ashore on to the tundra to nest, and ducks lay their eggs on the ground hidden in vegetation or under a rock. The drakes soon return to the sea, where they start to moult. When migrating, oldsquaws generally fly quite low in lines, rather than in any other organized formation. The females and young birds tend to migrate further south than the adult drakes.

IDENTIFICATION

- Black head, neck and chest, with white around the eyes and white underparts.

- More grey than brown on the wings.

- Long tail plumes.

- Ducks are smaller, and the sides of the face become white rather than black outside the breeding season.

FACT FILE

Distribution Breeds inland in parts of Iceland and Scandinavia. Moves to the coast in winter, including northern Scotland, Ireland and shores of the North Sea

Size 47cm/19in

Habitat Coastal waters and bays

Nest Hidden under a rock or in vegetation

Eggs 5–7, olive buff

Food Mainly marine invertebrates and crustaceans

Rivers, Lakes and Marshes

A wide variety of birds live by rivers and lakes, and in marshes. Birds of prey such as ospreys hunt in these freshwater habitats, swooping low over the water to seize fish. Other birds dive for their food, or probe into the wet mud with their bills for snails, worms and insects. The reedbeds offer good cover from predators and provide safe nesting places.

White Stork

Ciconia ciconia

This migratory bird spends the breeding season in Europe and North Africa, and the winter in warmer southern countries. The migration of white storks on their two flight paths in April each year – over the Strait of Gibraltar and further east over the Bosphorus – is a spectacular sight. They fly with their long necks extended and their legs trailing behind their bodies. These birds and their descendants often return year after year to the same nest site on the top of a building, adding more twigs each time to make a bulky structure. The number of white storks has declined in some areas due to drainage of their wetland habitat.

The white stork has long, shaggy throat and breast feathers.

The black flight feathers are a sharp contrast to the stork's white plumage.

IDENTIFICATION

- Large, tall, mainly white bird with prominent black areas on the back and wings.

- Long red bill and legs.

- Sexes are alike.

- Young birds are smaller with a dark tip to the bill.

FACT FILE

Distribution Summer visitor to much of mainland Europe. Winters in western and eastern parts of North Africa, depending on the flight path. Also occurs in Asia

Size 110cm/43in

Habitat Wetland areas

Nest Large platform of sticks, located off the ground

Eggs 3–5, chalky white

Food Amphibians, fish, small mammals and invertebrates

Eurasian Spoonbill

Platalea leucorodia

The spoonbill feeds mainly at night, leaving its daytime roost just before dusk to begin searching for food. As it wades, it sweeps its bill from side to side in the water. Anything edible is filtered through and trapped inside the slightly open, spoon-shaped tip. It can take up to four years for spoonbills to start nesting. Courting birds point their bills and preen each other. These birds can swim if they need to, but usually live in calm, shallow water. When resting, they may perch on one leg and tuck their bills over their backs.

▼*Spoonbills like to keep close together in small groups.*

The spoonbill uses its unique, highly specialized bill to sweep the water for fish and aquatic insects.

Long legs enable the spoonbill to wade into water up to 50cm/20in deep to feed.

IDENTIFICATION

- Highly distinctive bill is the major characteristic: long and black with an enlarged tip that is yellow-edged and shaped like a spoon.

- Has a crest of feathers on the back of the neck that is longer in the male than the female.

- Has an orange patch of plumage on the chest during the breeding season. Rest of the feathering is white.

- Legs are black.

- Young have a narrower bill that is light-coloured.

BIRDWATCH

Several features help you to spot this spoonbill as it flies past. One is its spatula-like bill. Another is the shape that it forms as it flies. Waders such as the heron fly with their head and neck in an S-shape, but a spoonbill extends its head and neck. Look out also for the black tips on its outer flight feathers.

FACT FILE

Distribution Breeds in northern temperate parts of Europe and Asia, as far east as China. Winters further south in tropical parts of Africa and South-east Asia. Indian birds are sedentary

Size 93cm/37in

Habitat Mudflats and marshes

Nest Stick platform off the ground

Eggs 3–4, white with brown markings

Food Fish, other aquatic creatures and vegetation

Grey Heron

Ardea cinerea

The grey heron hunts alone with a deadly combination of stealth and speed. It stands perfectly motionless at the water's edge, looking closely for the tiniest sign of movement in the water. It then strikes quickly, stabbing down its long, pointed bill to grab any fish or frog that swims within reach and swallowing it whole. During the winter months, when their freshwater habitats are frozen, grey herons often move to river estuaries in search of food. They may travel up to 30km/18 miles from their usual home territory to visit a good feeding site. Grey herons frequently nest in large colonies, with each male defending his small tree-top territory. Some breeding sites have been used by one generation of grey herons after another for several centuries.

The grey heron has a distinctive long black crest.

Plumage is mainly grey, with a white head and dark streaks on the long neck.

The grey heron's long, wide, rounded wings make these birds look really large when they are in flight.

Long legs are an advantage when stalking prey in deeper water.

IDENTIFICATION

- Long and powerful yellow bill.

- White head with black area and longer plumes coming off the back of the head.

- Long neck and chest are whitish with a black stripe down the centre.

- Wings are grey with black areas at the shoulder.

- Underparts are a lighter grey colour. Yellow legs.

- Sexes are alike.

- Young have browner plumage during their first winter.

BIRDWATCH

When resting, the grey heron sits with its head hunched into its shoulders. In spite of its large size, this bird can easily be overlooked because it remains so completely still and silent. Often, it will see you first, and will then stretch its neck in alarm and take flight. The heron frequently calls as it flies. Its harsh call may let you know that it is there long before you actually notice it in the air.

FACT FILE

Distribution Throughout most of Europe into Asia, apart from the far north. Also occurs in North Africa and ranges south, as far as the area around the Sahara Desert

Size 100cm/39in

Habitat Areas of water with reeds

Nest Platform of sticks built off the ground

Eggs 3–5, chalky blue

Food Fish and other aquatic vertebrates

Great Crested Grebe

Podiceps cristatus

Great crested grebes have short wings, so they cannot fly very well. Their legs are set well back on the body and this restricts their ability to move fast across open ground. They can swim quickly, however, thanks to the streamlined shape of their body, although their toes are not fully webbed, unlike those of waterfowl. They can also dive very effectively, often disappearing underwater if they feel threatened.

IDENTIFICATION

- Black from top of head to back.
- Brownish areas on sides in winter.
- In summer, black crest, with chestnut ruff at rear of head.
- Bill reddish pink.
- Sexes are alike.

The ruff-type facial feathers are used during the grebe's courting display.

FACT FILE

Distribution Europe east to China and southwards across much of Africa. Also Australia and New Zealand
Size 51cm/20in
Habitat Extensive reedy stretches of water
Nest Mound of reeds
Eggs 3–6, chalky white
Food Fish and various invertebrates

Water Rail

Rallus aquaticus

The water rail looks something like a small moorhen, but with a long red bill. It has an extensive range across most of Europe and Asia. It even survives in Iceland during the winter, thanks to the hot thermal springs, which never freeze. In some parts of their range, however, water rails migrate to warmer regions for the winter. Water rails are territorial when breeding and their chicks hatch with a covering of down.

The water rail has a prominent, long red bill.

FACT FILE

IDENTIFICATION

- Bluish-grey breast and sides of head. Narrow, brownish line over top of head down the back and wings. Long red bill.
- Black-and-white barring on the flanks and underparts.
- Short tail with pale buff underparts.
- Sexes are alike.

Distribution Extensive, from Iceland throughout most of Europe, south to North Africa and east across Asia to Siberia, China and Japan
Size 26cm/10in
Habitat: Reed beds in marshland and sedge
Nest Cup made of vegetation
Eggs 5–16, whitish with reddish-brown spotting
Food Mainly animal matter, but also some vegetation

Moorhen

Common moorhen *Gallinula chloropus*

Although it is a shy bird, the moorhen has become used to humans and can often be seen in parks and other public places where there is water. For most of the year moorhens form flocks of 15–30 birds, but during the breeding season they become very aggressive. If another bird comes too close, a moorhen may make a running attack on the intruder, with a flurry of wing- and leg-beating. Moorhens feed when swimming or when browsing on land. Their diet varies according to the season, but seeds are their main food. If danger threatens, moorhens either dive or swim underwater. They are good divers, remaining submerged by grasping underwater plants with their bills.

The moorhen's bill is a bright red colour, apart from the yellow tip.

▼ **This chick is being fed by its parent, but moorhen chicks are able to feed themselves within about three weeks.**

The greenish-yellow legs have a small red area at the top.

FACT FILE

Long toes with large claws allow the moorhen to walk over muddy ground and water plants.

IDENTIFICATION

- Slate-grey head, back and underparts. Underparts are a lighter grey.
- Bright red bill with yellow tip.
- Greyish-black wings.
- Prominent white line runs down the sides of the body.
- Area under the tail is white with a black central stripe.
- Greenish-yellow legs.
- Sexes are alike.

BIRDWATCH

The moorhen is very easily spotted in the water, with its bright red and yellow bill and jerking head movement as it swims. It is also the only waterfowl that has a red forehead. This, together with the distinctive white line that runs down each side of the body, distinguishes it from the coot. Another difference is that the young moorhen has less white on its throat than the young coot.

Distribution Very wide, from Great Britain east throughout Europe except for the far north. Occurs through much of Africa, especially southern parts, and also through much of South-east Asia and parts of the Americas

Size 30cm/12in

Habitat Ponds and other areas of water edged by dense vegetation

Nest Domed structure hidden in reeds

Eggs 2–17, buff to light green with dark markings

Food Omnivorous

Coot

Eurasian coot *Fulica atra*

In winter, coots gather in flocks on large stretches of waters that are unlikely to freeze over. They find food on land or dive into the water for pondweed. Stronger birds obtain their food by stealing from others. When breeding, pairs are very territorial, attacking chicks of other coots that venture too close, and even their own chicks, which they grab by the neck. Such behaviour is often described as tousling. The young respond by feigning death and this results in them being left alone.

The coot has a white bill with a white frontal plate.

IDENTIFICATION

- Sooty-grey, plump body. Black neck and head. White bill and frontal plate. White wing edge is evident in flight.

- Long toes have no webbing.

- Sexes are alike.

FACT FILE

Distribution From Great Britain east throughout Europe, except the far north, south into North Africa and east to Asia, as well as Australia and New Zealand

Size 42cm/16.5in

Habitat Still and also slow-flowing stretches of water

Nest Pile of reeds at the water's edge

Eggs 1–14, buff to brown with dark markings

Food Variety of plant and animal matter

Purple Swamp Hen

Porphyrio porphyrio

In Europe, the purple swamp hen has become scarce because of habitat changes. Many of the wetland areas in which it lives have been drained in recent years. Fortunately, in other parts of the world, such as the Nile Valley of Egypt, numbers have increased thanks to suitable habitats created by irrigation schemes. Purple swamp hens are most likely to be seen late in the day, when they venture out in search of food, often climbing reed stems. They are rather clumsy on short flights, running across the surface of the water to take off, and flying with their legs hanging down rather than being held against the body. Their calls include loud hooting, cackling, clucking and hoarse rippling notes.

The purple swamp hen's dull red bill has a bright red frontal plate.

The legs and toes are long.

IDENTIFICATION

- Vivid blue and purplish shades in the plumage. White undertail coverts. The wings may have a greenish hue.

- Red bill and plate, and pink-red legs.

- Sexes are alike.

FACT FILE

Distribution Southern Europe, sporadic locations in North Africa and southern parts of that continent. Also present in Asia, Australia and New Zealand

Size 50cm/20in

Habitat Reedy lakes and marshes

Nest Platform of vegetation just above the water

Eggs 2–7, whitish to green with dark spots

Food Mostly vegetarian

Curlew

Eurasian curlew *Numenius arquata*

The distinctive call note of the curlew, which gives the bird its name, can be heard some distance away. This wader flourishes over wide areas because it is able to adapt to new habitats. Curlews nest on open moorland, rough pasture or in a woodland clearing. Outside the breeding season, they are most likely to be seen in coastal areas, where they feed by probing in the sand with their bills. Elsewhere they use their bills to pick berries and catch snails.

In flight, the curlew's legs project beyond the tail.

The speckled brown plumage acts as camouflage when the curlew is sitting on its nest.

The curlew's unusually long, curved bill enables it to probe deep into mud to capture its prey.

There are larger dark areas on the curlew's wings.

Curlews have the very long legs that are typical of wading birds.

FACT FILE

Distribution Present throughout the year in the British Isles and adjacent areas of northern Europe. Also breeds widely elsewhere in Europe and Asia, migrating south to the Mediterranean and Africa in winter

Size 57cm/22in

Habitat Marshland, moorland and also coastal areas

Nest Scrape on the ground concealed by vegetation

Eggs 4, greenish brown with darker spots

Food Omnivorous

IDENTIFICATION

- Speckled plumage, with lighter ground colour on the throat and buff chest.

- Larger dark patterning on the wings.

- Underparts and rump are white.

- Cocks have plain-coloured heads, but hens' heads usually show a trace of a white stripe running down over the crown.

- Hens can also be distinguished by their longer bills, up to 15cm/6in long. Grey rather than buff plumage when not breeding.

BIRDWATCH

In flight, curlews look similar to young gulls. However, they can be identified by the bill shape and the way in which their legs project beyond the tail. Even when camouflaged in low-lying heathland, or among crops of wheat and barley, there is no mistaking the curlews' whistling cry.

Little Ringed Plover

Charadrius dubius

These plovers like to nest in areas with exposed gravel, where their coloration helps to camouflage them very effectively. Little ringed plovers migrate to Africa from their breeding grounds in Europe at the end of September and return the following March. They are more likely to be seen in coastal regions outside the breeding period. They do not tend to associate in mixed flocks with other waders, choosing instead to form small groups on their own. These birds may also be seen near temporarily flooded areas, including farmland.

There is strongly patterned colouring on the crown, the face and the neck.

IDENTIFICATION

- Broad black lines stretch across the forehead and from the bill back around the eye. A broader black band runs across the chest. Brown crown edged with white. White neck collar. The entire underparts are white.

- Legs are pinkish brown and the bill is black.

- The sexes are alike.

FACT FILE

Distribution Ranges from southern Scandinavia south across much of Europe, wintering in Africa. Also present in Asia
Size 18cm/7in
Habitat Sandy areas near fresh water
Nest Scrape on the ground
Eggs 3, stone-buff with dark markings
Food Invertebrates

Snipe

Common snipe *Gallinago gallinago*

These waders are very shy and mostly nocturnal in their feeding habits, probing damp ground with jerky movements of their long, stocky bills. If surprised in the open, snipes may freeze, but often they take off almost vertically, powering away and flying in a zigzag fashion, before plunging back down into suitable cover. In some parts of their range, such as the British Isles, snipe do not migrate. Those that live in more northerly latitudes, such as Iceland and Scandinavia, often migrate south to Africa to avoid severe winter weather, when the frozen ground makes it very difficult for them to find sufficient food.

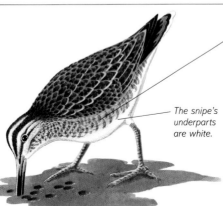

The chest and wings have dark mottled plumage.

The snipe's underparts are white.

IDENTIFICATION

- Pale buff stripe running down the centre of the crown, with buff stripes above and below the eyes.

- White stripes down the wing. White border to the rear of the wing. Underparts white. Dark mottling on chest and wings.

- Long bill may be larger in hens.

- Sexes otherwise alike.

FACT FILE

Distribution Ranges from Iceland both west across North America and east through Europe and Asia. May migrate to southerly latitudes for the winter
Size 28cm/11in
Habitat Marshland and wet pasture
Nest Scrape on the ground
Eggs 3, greenish buff with dark markings
Food Invertebrates

Whooper Swan

Cygnus cygnus

Some Icelandic whooper swans do not migrate, but the majority of these birds undertake regular migrations, so they are likely to be seen in southern Europe only during the winter months. They often live around inland areas of water at this time, such as the Black and Caspian seas. Pairs mate in March and April and nest on their own, and the young chicks fly alongside their parents on the journey south. In the winter, whooper swans may sometimes invade agricultural areas, where they eat a wide range of foods varying from potatoes to acorns, although generally they prefer to feed on aquatic vegetation.

▼ *Graceful flight, with slow and regular wingbeats, is characteristic of all species of swans.*

Swans use their extremely long neck to reach and feed off water plants below the surface.

The yellow bill distinguishes the whooper swan from the mute swan.

The adult swan has pure white plumage.

IDENTIFICATION

- Body plumage is white, although it may sometimes be stained.

- Base of the bill is yellow, extending as far down as the nostrils, and the tip is black.

- Legs and feet are grey.

- Hens are a little smaller.

- Young birds have pinkish rather than yellow bases to their bills. Their grey upperparts become browner in colour until the second year, when adult colouring is attained.

BIRDWATCH

The whooper swan differs from the mute swan in having a bill with a yellow base, not an orange tip. While on the ground it holds its neck upright. A whooper swan's wings make a whistling sound in flight, while a mute swan's wings throb. The whooper swan also has a noisier call.

FACT FILE

Distribution Iceland and Scandinavia east to Siberia. Overwinters further south

Size 165cm/65in

Habitat Ponds and lakes, typically in wooded areas. Often overwinters close to the coast

Nest Mounds of plant matter, often moss

Eggs 3–7, pale green

Food Vegetation

Mute Swan

Cygnus olor

These swans live in a wide range of habitats, and may even venture on to the sea, although they do not stray far from the shore. They prefer to feed on aquatic vegetation. They rarely dive, but use their long necks to dabble under the surface of the water to obtain food. Sometimes they will graze on short grass, and in parks will eat foods that are given to them, such as grain and bread. Mute swan pairs are territorial when breeding, and the male swan, called the cob, will try to drive away people who venture too close with fierce movements of its wings.

A black area stretches from the eyes to the base of the bill.

IDENTIFICATION

- Mainly white; may be traces of staining on the head and neck. Bill orange, with a black knob at base.
- Legs and feet are blackish.
- Pens (females) are smaller with a less pronounced knob on the bill.
- Young birds are browner.

FACT FILE

Distribution Resident in the British Isles and adjacent areas of western Europe, and often found living in a semi-domesticated state. Also occurs in parts of Asia. Localized introduced populations in South Africa, the eastern USA, Australia and New Zealand
Size 160cm/63in
Habitat Larger stretches of fresh water and estuaries
Nest Large pile of heaped-up aquatic vegetation
Eggs 5–7, pale green
Food Mainly vegetation

Canada Goose

Branta canadensis

There are several different races of Canada goose and they all differ a little in plumage and size. Some are scarcely bigger than a mallard, while others are twice that size. The number of Canada geese in Europe has grown considerably, especially in farming areas, where flocks descend to feed on crops during winter once other food has become scarce. When migrating, flocks fly in a clear V-shaped formation. Like many waterfowl, Canada geese are not able to fly when they are moulting (around June), but they take readily to the water at this time and can dive if necessary to escape danger. The geese prefer to graze on land, returning to the relative safety of the water during the hours of darkness.

A small area of white plumage runs in a stripe from behind the eyes to under the throat.

FACT FILE

Distribution Throughout the far north of the Americas, wintering in the southern USA. European population occurs in the British Isles and elsewhere in north-western Europe
Size 55–110cm/ 22–43in
Habitat Very variable, but usually near water
Nest Vegetation on the ground
Eggs 4–7, whitish
Food Vegetarian

IDENTIFICATION

- Black head and neck. White stripe around face. White at base of neck.
- Wings are dark brown and there is white on the abdomen. Brown chest.
- Legs and feet are blackish.
- Sexes are alike.

Snow Goose

Anser caerulescens

Snow geese are a fairly common sight in north-western parts of Europe during the winter months. They are especially attracted to farmland, where there is plenty of grazing. Snow goose pairs remain together for life and in the spring they fly north together to breed and raise their young in the Arctic tundra. They nest in huge colonies of up to 200,000 pairs. Both birds help to build the nest, and the female sits on the eggs while the male watches out for predators, such as the Arctic fox. The young geese quickly begin feeding themselves and grow rapidly, so that in little more than a month they are ready for the journey south. There are two forms, or "phases" of this goose. One is mostly white. The other, which is much less common, has blue-grey coloration.

◀ *The rarer blue form of snow goose.*

The blue snow goose has dark grey plumage tinged with blue on the back and wing.

The white form of ▶ *the snow goose.*

The pink bill is quite short, with sharp, serrated cutting edges for grazing on the tundra vegetation.

The white snow goose's plumage is dazzling white, except for the black wing tips.

IDENTIFICATION

- Blue snow geese are dark bluish-grey, with white heads and white borders to some wing feathers.

- Young birds of the blue colour phase (or form) have dark heads.

- White snow geese are almost entirely white, with dark primary wing feathers.

- Young birds of the white phase have greyish markings on their heads.

- Sexes are alike.

BIRDWATCH

This is an easy goose to identify. Black wing tips distinguish the white form from swans and albino (all white) geese of other species. The blue form differs from other grey geese in having a white head. You may spot a lone snow goose in a large flock of grazing grey geese.

FACT FILE

Distribution Mainly Arctic North America, Greenland and north-eastern Siberia, but frequently overwinters in Great Britain and nearby coastal areas of north-western Europe

Size 84cm/33in

Habitat Tundra and coastal lowland agricultural areas

Nest Depression lined with vegetation

Eggs 4–10, whitish

Food Vegetarian

Lapwing

Northern lapwing *Vanellus vanellus*

Lapwings are also called peewits because of the sound of their call. In winter, flocks of these birds are a common sight in farmland areas, where they comb the ploughed soil for invertebrates. During prolonged spells of severe winter weather, when freshwater areas become frozen, they congregate in estuaries. In early spring the flocks break up into breeding pairs. Attracting the female by scraping the ground and showing off his chestnut undertail feathers, the male makes several shallow scrapes in the soil from which the female chooses. She lines the hollow with dried grass and leaves before laying her eggs.

The lapwing is easily recognized by its long crest.

FACT FILE

Distribution Occurs from southern Scandinavia southwards to the Mediterranean, and migrates eastwards as far as Japan. Also occurs in North Africa and may also be seen further south

Size 30cm/12in

Habitat Marshland and farmland

Nest Scrape on the ground

Eggs 4, light brown with dark markings

Food Mainly invertebrates

IDENTIFICATION

- Long black crest, with black on the face, separated by a white streak in hens.

- Wings are dark green, with a grey-green area on the neck. Underparts are white, apart from chestnut undertail coverts.

- White cheeks broken by a black line.

Ruddy Shelduck

Tadorna ferruginea

Most of these shelducks migrate to warmer places for the winter, but some remain in the same place all year. Occasionally, they are seen well outside their natural range, in countries as far apart as Iceland, Oman and Kenya. Ruddy shelducks are quite noisy birds, and the calls of drakes are of a higher pitch than those of hens. Ruddy shelducks prefer stretches of water in open countryside, so that they can graze on the surrounding vegetation. Huge flocks may assemble in some areas where conditions are favourable for feeding after the breeding season has finished.

The tail and flight feathers are black.

The drake's black neck ring is less apparent outside the breeding season.

FACT FILE

Distribution North-western Africa, south-western Europe and Asia. Overwinters in eastern Africa

Size 70cm/27.5in

Habitat Inland, can be some distance from any water

Nest Down-lined and under cover

Eggs 8–15, creamy white

Food Aquatic creatures and plant matter

IDENTIFICATION

- Head is cinnamon-coloured, with whitish area around the eyes. Black neck ring. Rest of the body orange-brown. Black tail with green gloss to black feathers on the rump.

- Bill, legs and feet are black.

- Black flight feathers. White under the wings.

- Hens do not have a neck collar.

49

Mallard

Anas platyrhynchos

These ducks are a common sight on stretches of water in towns and cities, such as rivers and canals. They may gather in quite large flocks, especially outside the breeding season, but they are most evident in the spring, when groups of unpaired males chase potential mates. The nest is often built close to water and is frequently hidden under vegetation, especially in urban areas. These birds feed on water, upending themselves or dabbling at the surface, and also on land.

The metallic-green head of the mallard drake (male) is one of the most easily recognized features among British and European birds.

The female ▶ mallard.

◀ The male mallard.

The female has dull brown colouring.

The mallard drake has a highly distinctive white ring right around his neck.

The duck and the drake both have a distinctive bluish patch on the wing.

The drake has very striking coloration, unlike the female mallard.

IDENTIFICATION

- The head of the drake (male) is a metallic green, with a white ring around the neck.

- The chest of the drake is brownish-purple with grey underparts.

- Bluish patch in the wing of the drake, most evident in flight, bordered by black-and-white stripes.

- Hen is brownish buff overall with darker patterning, and has same wing markings as the drake.

- Hen's bill is orange, whereas that of male in eclipse plumage (outside the breeding season) is yellow.

BIRDWATCH

The mallard is an extremely familiar duck. There is a marked difference between the male with its bright plumage and the dull brown female. The drake is easily recognized by its green head, narrow white collar and dark purple-brown breast. The female makes a loud, harsh "quack", rather like a farmyard duck.

FACT FILE

Distribution Occurs throughout the northern hemisphere, including North Africa, and is resident through western parts of Europe

Size 60cm/24in

Habitat Open areas of water

Nest Scrape lined with down feathers

Eggs 7–16, buff to greyish green

Food Plant matter and some invertebrates

Shoveler

Northern shoveler *Anas clypeata*

The broad bill of these waterfowl enables them to feed more easily in shallow water. They swim with their bill open, trailing it through the water to catch invertebrates, and also forage for food by upending and by catching insects on reeds. Shovelers choose wet ground, often some distance from open water, as a nesting site, where the female retreats from the attention of other drakes. Like the young of other waterfowl, these young ducks take to the water soon after hatching.

The shoveler is easily identified by its broad black, shovel-like bill.

IDENTIFICATION

- Very broad black bill.
- Dark metallic-green head and orange eye.
- White chest, chestnut-brown flanks and belly, and a black area around the tail.
- Back and wings are black and white.
- Broad blue wing stripe.
- Hens are predominantly brownish.
- Yellowish edges on the bill and paler area of plumage on the sides of the tail.

FACT FILE

Distribution Widely distributed right across the northern hemisphere, spending winters as far south as central Africa
Size 52cm/20in
Habitat Shallow coastal and freshwater areas
Nest Down-lined scrape
Eggs 8–12, green to buff white
Food Plant matter and aquatic invertebrates

Pochard

Aythya ferina

These diving ducks are most likely to be seen in areas of open water, where they often dive for food. They prefer stretches of water where there are islands, as these provide relatively secure nesting sites, particularly if there is overhanging vegetation. Pairs stay together during the nesting period. After that, pochards form larger flocks, sometimes moving away from lakes and similar stretches of still water to nearby rivers, especially in cold weather when it is likely that ice will form on the water's surface.

The pochard's reddish eyes are a distinctive feature.

Black feathers are replaced by grey ones outside the breeding season.

FACT FILE

Distribution Resident in parts of western Europe, extending eastwards into Asia and overwintering as far south as Africa
Size 49cm/19in
Habitat Marshland and lakes
Nest Down-lined and under cover
Eggs 6–14, green-grey
Food Aquatic creatures and plant matter

IDENTIFICATION

- Chestnut-brown head and neck, with black chest and a broad grey band encircling the wings and body. Black tail feathers.
- Black areas are replaced by greyish tone in eclipse plumage (outside breeding season).
- Hens are significantly duller: a brown head with buff areas and a pale stripe extending back from the eye.

51

Kingfisher

Common kingfisher *Alcedo atthis*

The kingfisher is considered by many people to be one of Europe's most beautiful birds. It is a highly specialized hunter, plunging into rivers and streams to catch fish. A protective membrane covers its eyes as it enters the water. Its wings provide propulsion, and having seized the fish in its bill, the bird then darts out of the water and back on to its perch with its catch. This movement happens incredibly fast, with the whole process taking little more than a second. The kingfisher first stuns the fish by hitting it on the perch and then swallows it head first. It regurgitates the bones and indigestible parts of its meal later.

Kingfishers ▶ dive at speed into the water to catch their prey unawares.

The powerful bill is ideal for grasping fish and snatching them rapidly out of the water.

The head is large in relation to the rest of the body.

The kingfisher perches motionless on a branch while it looks out for fish in the water below.

FACT FILE

IDENTIFICATION

- Bluish-green colour that extends over the head and wings.

- Back is pale blue, and a blue flash is also present on the cheeks.

- An area under the throat and across the back of the neck is white.

- Patches on the cheeks, and also the underparts of the body, are orange.

- Bill is black.

- In hens, the bill is reddish at the base of the lower bill.

BIRDWATCH

Despite its bright colours, the kingfisher is not easy to see. Its blue-green back and wings actually form good camouflage as it flies low over water. However, it makes loud, shrill, whistling, piping and trilling calls. These are unlike any other bird's calls and often give away its presence.

Distribution Occurs across most of Europe, apart from much of Scandinavia. Also present in North Africa and ranges eastwards through southern Asia to the Solomon Islands
Size 18cm/7in
Habitat Near to slow-flowing water
Nest Tunnel excavated in sandy bank
Eggs 6–10, white
Food Small fish, aquatic insects, molluscs and crustaceans

Swallow

Barn swallow *Hirundo rustica*

The return of
swallows to their
breeding grounds in
Europe is one of the
welcomed signs of spring.
Pairs return to the same
nest each year, but they
do not migrate together.
Cock birds arrive back
before their partners and
jealously guard the site from
would-be rivals. Although swallows
sometimes use traditional nesting
sites, such as caves or hollow
trees, they also build their nests
inside buildings, such as barns,
choosing a site close to the eaves.
It can take as many as 1,000 trips
to collect damp mud, carried back
in the bill, to complete a new nest.

With its forked tail and long pointed wings, the swallow can perform graceful acrobatics in the air.

IDENTIFICATION

- Chestnut forehead and throat, dark blue head and back, narrow dark blue band across the chest.

- Wings are blackish.

- Underparts are white with long streamers on the tail feathers.

- Sexes are alike.

FACT FILE

Distribution Throughout most of the northern hemisphere. European swallows overwinter in sub-Saharan Africa
Size 19cm/7.5in
Habitat Open country, close to water
Nest Made of mud, and built off the ground
Eggs 4–5, white with red and grey spotting
Food Invertebrates

Sand Martin

African sand martin; bank swallow *Riparia riparia*

In the summer months, sand martins are
usually seen relatively close to lakes and
other stretches of water, often swooping
down to catch invertebrates. They are
likely to be nesting in colonies nearby,
in tunnels that they excavate on
suitable sandy banks. The nesting
chamber is lined with grass,
seaweed or similar material,
and the eggs are laid on top
of a softer bed of feathers.
When the young birds leave
the nest, they stay in groups
with other chicks, until their parents
return to feed them. Parents recognize
their offspring by their distinctive calls.
If danger threatens, the repetitive alarm
calls of the adult sand martins cause the
young to rush back to the protection of
the nesting tunnels.

◀ *The sand martin's nesting tunnel may extend back for up to 1m/3ft.*

The sand martin has long wings and a forked tail.

IDENTIFICATION

- Predominantly brown, with white plumage on the throat, separated from the white underparts by a brown band across the breast.

- Long flight feathers.

- Small dark bill.

- Sexes are alike.

FACT FILE

Distribution Across Europe and Asia to North America. Overwinters in sub-Saharan Africa and South America
Size 11cm/4in
Habitat Open country, close to water
Nest Holes and tunnels in sandbanks
Eggs 3–4, white
Food Invertebrates

Osprey

Pandion haliaetus

The osprey has one of the greatest ranges of any bird. In many areas, especially in Europe, ospreys are migratory, and the birds head south to Africa for the duration of the northern winter. During the breeding season the male osprey performs dramatic displays to attract a mate, flying rapidly upwards to a height of 300m/1,000ft or more, carrying a fish in his talons. Ospreys feed on stretches of fresh water, on estuaries and even the open sea, swooping to grab fish from just below the water's surface using their powerful talons. They are capable of carrying fish weighing up to 300g/11oz.

▲ *The osprey builds its nest high above the ground, in a tree-top or on a crag.*

BIRDWATCH

Ospreys are very distinctive birds. Large, with long legs and strong talons, they hold their long, slender wings in a shallow "M" shape in flight. They are unpopular in some areas because they prey on fish stocks. Their numbers have been reduced by hunting and pesticide poisoning.

The osprey strikes by plunging down with its wings swept back.

FACT FILE

IDENTIFICATION

- Brown stripes running across the eyes down over the back and wings.

- Eyes are yellow.

- Top of the head and underparts are white, with brown stripes across the breast, which are most obvious in the hens.

- Tall, upright stance, powerful grey legs and talons.

- Hens significantly heavier than cocks.

Curving talons and small hooks under its toes help the osprey to grasp slippery fish.

Distribution Global, with European ospreys ranging from parts of Scandinavia west to the British Isles and south to the Iberian Peninsula and other areas in Europe. Widely distributed in the winter in Africa south of the Sahara

Size 58cm/23in

Habitat Close to stretches of water

Nest Platform of sticks in a tree

Eggs 3, white with darker markings

Food Fish

Western Marsh Harrier

Swamp harrier *Circus aeruginosus*

Unlike many birds of prey, this harrier is a truly opportunistic hunter. It raids the nests of other birds, as well as catching the birds themselves, and also hunts mammals, such as rabbits, by swooping on them in the open. Its food varies, partly depending on its range, and may change throughout the year. During the winter, even the carcasses of dead whales washed ashore in coastal areas may feature in its diet. In Asia, these birds tend to migrate southwards at this time of year. Pairs regularly return to the same nest site in the following spring.

▼ *The coloration and markings of the various different forms of this bird vary widely. In some forms, the males are generally darker than the females.*

The female marsh harrier is larger than the male.

Male marsh harriers often have plainer coloration.

IDENTIFICATION

- Plumage varies according to the race.
- Head is brownish with white streaks.
- Darker streaking on a buff chest.
- The abdomen is entirely brown.
- Wings are brown with rufous (reddish) edging to the feathers.
- White and grey areas are also apparent.
- Tail is pale greyish.
- Hens are larger than male birds, with yellowish-cream colouring on the head, throat and shoulder.
- Young birds resemble hens but have darker shoulder markings.

BIRDWATCH

The swamp harrier is larger than other harriers of the same region, and its plumage is largely brown, rather than grey. It has broader, more rounded wings, and is less graceful in flight. The male is nearer to the female in size than other harriers. Females and young birds can be distinguished from same-sized birds of prey by the paler head.

FACT FILE

Distribution Recently seen in Ireland – near lakes and stretches of fresh water – and also found in eastern England. Present on the European mainland, but it is not seen throughout the year in all areas here. Range extends south to Africa and east through Asia

Size 48–56cm/19–22in

Habitat Marshland and nearby open country

Nest Pile of reeds in a secluded reedbed

Eggs 2–7, pale bluish-white

Food Birds, plus other small vertebrates

Woodland

During the warm months of the year, woodland is an ideal habitat for birds. It provides a wide range of food, excellent cover and a variety of nesting sites. During the winter months life here can become much harsher. Once the leaves have fallen, the birds are more conspicuous and food becomes scarce. Survival becomes even harder if snow covers the ground.

Barn Owl

Tyto alba

Although mainly a nocturnal species, the barn owl sometimes shows itself during daylight. This is most likely when the bird is feeding young, or in very cold weather when hunting is difficult. It may be seen in open country, swooping over farmland, snatching bats from the air or dropping down on to voles on the ground. The males utter harsh screeches to warn off other owls, and defend their territory aggressively with aerial fights. Barn owls pair for life, which can be more than 20 years. The female lays her eggs directly on to roof timbers or in a bare tree cavity. She alone incubates the clutch, but she is fed by the male.

IDENTIFICATION

■ Very pale in colour, with whitish, heart-shaped face and underparts, although in northern, central and eastern parts of Europe, the underparts have a decidedly yellowish-orange tone.

■ Top of the head and wings are greyish with spots evident.

■ Eyes are black.

■ Male birds are often paler than females.

The female lays an egg every two or three days and the young hatch at similar intervals, resulting in a size difference between the chicks.

FACT FILE

Distribution Worldwide. Throughout western Europe, Africa (apart from the Sahara) and the Middle East

Size 39cm/15in

Habitat Prefers relatively open countryside

Nest Hollow tree or inside a building

Eggs 4–7, white

Food Amphibians, voles, bats and invertebrates

Tawny Owl

Strix aluco

The distinctive "hoo-hoo-hoohoo" call of this bird reveals its presence, even when it is hard to spot due to its dark colouring. It prefers old woodland, where trees are big enough to provide cavities. Tawny owls also use nesting boxes, which have helped to increase their numbers in some areas. Nocturnal by nature, they may hunt by day when they have chicks in the nest. Young tawny owls are fed by their parents for a couple of months.

IDENTIFICATION

- Tawny brown with white markings on wings; darker streaks over wings and body.
- Distinctive white stripes above the facial disc, which is almost plain brown.
- The bill is yellowish brown.
- Sexes are similar, although females are generally larger and heavier.

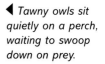

◀ *Tawny owls sit quietly on a perch, waiting to swoop down on prey.*

FACT FILE

Distribution Across Europe (not Ireland) to Scandinavia and east to Asia. Also occurs in western North Africa
Size 43cm/17in
Habitat Ancient temperate woodland
Nest Tree holes
Eggs 2–9, white
Food Small mammals, birds and invertebrates

The tail feathers have brown bars.

Eagle Owl

Eurasian eagle owl *Bubo bubo*

The scientific name of the eagle owl – *Bubo bubo* – reflects the sound of its calls, which can be heard from quite a distance. A pair will call alternately before mating, and the call notes·of the female are higher in pitch. Despite their large size, eagle owls fly quietly and may even soar. Formidable hunters, they go after large, potentially dangerous quarry, including buzzards and herons. However, they often resort to catching earthworms and fish, as well as eating carrion, when hunting opportunities are limited.

IDENTIFICATION

- Brownish with dark markings on the wings. Underparts are buff brown with streaking most evident on the breast.
- Prominent ear tufts, black bill and orange eyes.
- Females are often slightly bigger.

◀There are at least 13 different types of eagle owl.

FACT FILE

Distribution Throughout southern Europe, north to Scandinavia and east across Asia. Small populations in parts of western Europe and western North Africa
Size 73cm/29in
Habitat Rocky areas, relatively open country
Nest Cliff ledges or sometimes on the ground
Eggs 1–4, white
Food Mammals and birds

Snowy Owl

Nyctea scandiaca

The plumage of these owls enables them to blend in well in the tundra region where they live. In this harsh environment, the success of the snowy owl is related to the availability of prey. Numbers increase when there are plenty of lemmings. Once the lemming population declines, however, so does that of the snowy owl. Breeding opportunities are less, so that pairs may not nest at all in some years. Adult birds are forced to abandon their usual territories and fly south in search of other food sources. Unusually, snowy owls are active during the day.

The male is almost totally white, with just a few dark flecks on his plumage.

IDENTIFICATION

- Males are white with yellow eyes and feathering down to the claws.

- Females have brown barring all over their bodies apart from their faces, which are white.

- Young are similar to females.

FACT FILE

Distribution Circumpolar in the northern hemisphere, moving further south in winter
Size 65cm/25.5in
Habitat Woodland, extending to the tundra
Nest Scrape on the ground
Eggs 3–11, white
Food Mainly lemmings; also birds, invertebrates and fish

Great Grey Owl

Strix nebulosa

These owls travel extensively. Much of their movement is triggered by the availability of food, especially voles, which they hunt almost exclusively during the breeding season. Pairs of great grey owls will often take over nests that have been abandoned by other birds of prey, such as buzzards, although they sometimes nest on the ground. The number of eggs in the clutch depends on the availability of food. Breeding is therefore related to fluctuations in the vole population.

Concentric rings are clearly visible on this owl's facial disc.

IDENTIFICATION

- Plumage coloration consists mainly of grey streaking and barring on a white background.

- Yellowish bill, with a blackish patch beneath; facial disc with concentric rings.

- Tail is relatively long.

- Females are larger in size.

FACT FILE

Distribution In the eastern forested parts of northern Europe, as far west as the Baltic region and parts of Scandinavia. Also found across northern Asia and also North America
Size 69cm/27in
Habitat Coniferous forest
Nest Often consists of a platform of sticks
Eggs 3–6, white
Food Small vertebrates, especially voles

Magpie

Common magpie *Pica pica*

This bold and garrulous bird is very common in Europe. Magpies are often blamed for the decline of songbirds because of their habit of raiding the nests of other birds. They are usually seen in small groups, although pairs will nest on their own. If a predator such as a cat ventures close to the nest, there will be a considerable commotion. Other magpies in the neighbourhood will join in to harry the unfortunate cat. Magpies sometimes take an equally direct approach when seeking food, chasing other birds, gulls in particular, to make them drop their food. Magpies are quite agile when walking, holding their long tails up as they move. Their flight is a series of rapid flaps and short glides.

Depending on the light, you can sometimes see a green gloss on the magpie's black plumage.

IDENTIFICATION

- Black head, upper breast, back, rump and tail, with a broad white patch around the abdomen.

- Broad white wing stripe and dark blue areas on folded wings.

- Sexes are alike; the male may have a longer tail.

FACT FILE

Distribution Much of Europe and south to North Africa. Also present in parts of Asia and North America
Size 51cm/20in
Habitat Trees with surrounding open areas
Nest Dome-shaped pile of sticks
Eggs 2–8, bluish green with darker markings
Food Omnivorous

Jay

Eurasian jay *Garrulus glandarius*

The jay is a common woodland bird in Europe. Secretive by nature, it rarely shows itself for long in the open, although it often reveals its presence by its harsh, scolding calls. Jays eat a variety of food according to the season, and feed on the ground and in the trees. Their diet includes caterpillars, worms, spiders and small rodents. During the summer, they may raid the nests of other birds, taking eggs and chicks. In autumn, they store acorns and other seeds, which help to sustain them through the winter when the ground may be covered in snow. A pair of jays may form a bond for life. Both birds build the nest, which is small and flat, high up in a tree.

The black facial stripe looks rather like a moustache.

FACT FILE

IDENTIFICATION

- Pinkish brown; greyer on the wings.

- Streaking on the head.

- Black stripe above white throat.

- White rump and undertail area.

- Tail is dark.

- Wings have white stripe and black and blue markings on the sides.

- Sexes are alike.

Distribution Throughout most of Europe (except Scotland and the extreme north of Scandinavia). Also present in North Africa and Asia
Size 35cm/14in
Habitat Woodland
Nest Platform of twigs
Eggs 3–7, bluish green with dense speckling
Food Omnivorous

Rook

Corvus frugilegus

These highly social birds nest in colonies, partly because they inhabit areas of open countryside where there are few trees available. There is, however, a strong bond between each pair. The rookery serves as the group's centre, which makes them vulnerable to human persecution. But although they eat corn, they are valued for consuming invertebrates. The rook's bill is adapted to digging in the ground to extract invertebrates, especially cranefly ("daddy-long-legs") larvae. Outside the breeding season, rooks may associate with jackdaws, crows and ravens, as an alternative to the rookery may be used as a roosting site at this time.

The rook is the only large black bird with a bare – unfeathered – facial patch (on its face and chin).

IDENTIFICATION

- Entirely black plumage, with a pointed bill that has bare grey skin at its base.
- Rooks have a flatter forehead than crows and a peak to the crown.
- Sexes are alike.

FACT FILE

Distribution Throughout Europe east to Asia. Some populations move south in the winter to the northern Mediterranean
Size 49cm/19in
Habitat Close to farmland
Nest Made of sticks built in trees
Eggs 2–7, bluish green with dark markings
Food Omnivorous, but mainly invertebrates

Raven

Common raven *Corvus corax*

The loud croaking calls are a foolproof way of identifying the raven. Its large size is also a good identifier. Ravens are the largest members of the crow family in the northern hemisphere. Those found in the far north are larger than those occurring further south. The impression of bulk is reinforced by their shaggy throat feathers. Pairs occupy fairly large territories, and even outside the breeding season they tend not to gather in large flocks. When searching for food, ravens are able to fly quite effortlessly over long distances, flapping their wings slowly.

A small number of ravens live at The Tower of London.

IDENTIFICATION

- Very large in size with a powerful, curved bill.
- Entirely black plumage.
- Wedge-shaped tail in flight, when the flight feathers stand out, creating a fingered appearance at the tips.
- Males often larger than females.

FACT FILE

Distribution Mainly south-western Europe and North Africa. North to Scandinavia and east throughout most of northern Asia. Also present in North America, Greenland, Iceland and the British Isles
Size 67cm/26in
Habitat Relatively open country
Nest Bulky, and made of sticks
Eggs 3–7, bluish with darker spots
Food Carrion

Great Spotted Woodpecker

Picoides major

These woodpeckers are likely to be seen in both coniferous and deciduous woodland habitats, especially in areas where the trees are mature enough for the birds to excavate chambers for roosting and nesting. Their powerful bill enables them to extract grubs concealed under the bark. They can also extract the seeds from pine cones using "anvils", which may be existing tree holes, as vices to hold the cones fast and gain more leverage for their bills.

The sharp, very strong bill of the woodpecker lets it drill into tree bark in search of food.

Unlike the male, the female does not have a red area on the back of the head.

Both sexes have the red area under the tail.

Male (right) ▶
and female (left)
woodpeckers.

There is a prominent white patch on each of the wings.

IDENTIFICATION

- A black area runs from the bill around the sides of the neck and links with a red area at the back.

- Wings and upper tail are predominantly black, although there is a white area on the wings and barring on the flight feathers.

- There is a deep red area beneath the tail and large white spots on the underside of the tail.

- Hens lack the red area at the back of the head.

BIRDWATCH

Woodpeckers have a number of instantly recognizable features that enable them to grip on to the bark of the trees on which they feed. Their feet have strong claws, and a pair of toes facing forwards and another backwards. The legs are short so that the body is held close to the trunk. The tail has a number of extremely strong, stiff feathers, which woodpeckers use to brace themselves while searching for grubs and insects.

FACT FILE

Distribution Most of Europe (except Ireland and the far north of Scandinavia). Also found in North Africa. Ranges east into Asia
Size 25cm/10in
Habitat Woodland
Nest Tree hollows
Eggs 5–7, white
Food Invertebrates, eggs and seeds

Cuckoo

Common cuckoo *Cuculus canorus*

The distinctive call of the common cuckoo is one of the best-loved early signs of spring in Europe. Adult cuckoos have an unusual ability to feed on hairy caterpillars, which are often plentiful in woodland areas through much of the summer. Common cuckoos are parasitic in their breeding habits, with hens laying single eggs in the nests of other smaller birds, such as wagtails, hedge sparrows and meadow pipits. The unsuspecting hosts hatch a monster in their midst, with the cuckoo chick throwing eggs or potential rivals out of the nest in order to monopolize the food supply. The adult cuckoos leave Europe in July to winter in warm central or southern Africa. Reared by its foster parents, the young cuckoo leaves between August and September – several weeks later than its real parents – and yet is still able to find its way to the regular wintering area it has never seen before.

BIRDWATCH

In flight, the cuckoo, with its long, pointed wings and grey-flecked underparts, can be confused with a sparrowhawk. This mimicry may be deliberate – to frighten a smaller bird off its nest, so that the cuckoo can lay her own egg there. However, it can always be identified by the graduated tail, with white spots and tips.

Adult males keep their bills closed when calling.

The graduated tail distinguishes the cuckoo from a sparrowhawk.

FACT FILE

Distribution Across Europe and east to Asia. Also present in North Africa. Northern European birds overwinter in eastern and southern parts of Africa, while Asiatic birds range out to the Philippines

Size 36cm/14in

Habitat Wide range, thanks to host species

Nest Lays eggs in other birds' nests

Eggs 1 per nest, resembles those of the host bird

Food Invertebrates, including caterpillars

IDENTIFICATION

- Grey head, upper chest, wings and tail, and black edging to the white feathers of the underparts.

- In hens this barring extends virtually up to the throat, offset against a more yellowish background.

- Some hens belong to a brown colour type, with reddish feathering replacing grey, and black barring on the upperparts.

▲ *The cuckoo chick usually hatches first and pushes the other eggs from the nest.*

Great Spotted Cuckoo

Clamator glandarius

The great spotted cuckoo has an easily identifiable crest on its head.

These lively cuckoos hunt for invertebrates in trees and on the ground, hopping along rather clumsily. Very bold by nature, they lay their eggs in the nests of magpies and starlings. The hen usually removes any eggs that are already present in the host bird's nest before laying, but if any remain and hatch, the nestlings are reared alongside the young cuckoos. Their relatively large size and noisy nature make these cuckoos quite conspicuous, particularly after the breeding period, when they form flocks.

IDENTIFICATION

- Silver-grey head with a slight crest.

- Grey neck, back and wings, with white spots over the wings. Pale yellow plumage under the throat extending to the upper breast. Remainder of underparts are white.

- Sexes are alike, although their song notes are different.

- Young birds are much darker – black rather than grey with rusty brown flight feathers.

FACT FILE

Distribution Ranges throughout southern Europe from Spain to Iran in Asia. Migrates to north-eastern and southern Africa

Size 39cm/15in

Habitat Fairly open woodland areas

Nest Lays eggs in other birds' nests

Eggs 1 per nest, resembles those of the host bird

Food Invertebrates

Nightjar

European nightjar *Caprimulgus europaeus*

The nightjar's mottled plumage provides good camouflage in daytime.

The nightjar is a regular summertime visitor to Europe. Its nocturnal habits make it difficult to observe, but it has a distinctive call that has been likened to the croaking of a frog or the noise of a machine. The calls are uttered for long periods and carry over a distance of up to 1km/0.6m. These birds spend much of their time resting on the ground during the daytime, but are sufficiently agile to catch moths and beetles in flight after dark. Nightjars may sometimes be seen hunting night-flying invertebrates. If food is plentiful, a pair may nest twice in succession before migrating south for the winter.

IDENTIFICATION

- Fine bill.

- Long wings.

- Greyish-brown mottled appearance overall, with some black areas too, especially near the shoulder.

- White areas below the eyes and on the wings, although white spots on the wings are seen only in male birds.

FACT FILE

Distribution Europe and North Africa, east to Asia. Northern European birds overwinter in central and southern parts of Africa, and those found in the south migrate to western Africa

Size 28cm/11in

Habitat Heathland and fairly open woodland

Nest Scrape on the ground

Eggs 2, buff with darker markings

Food Invertebrates

Open Countryside

Birds of prey are most likely to be seen gliding across open pasture or moorland. Their keen eyesight enables them to spot prey on the ground below. Smaller birds, such as the swift and the flycatcher, hawk insects on the wing. Many birds that live in the open countryside, for example quails and ptarmigans, rely on their colouring to conceal their presence.

Golden Eagle

Aquila chrysaetos

These eagles generally inhabit remote areas away from people, where they are likely to be left undisturbed. When seen in flight, the golden eagle's head looks relatively small compared to its broad tail and large, square-ended wings. Although it has some yapping call notes not unlike those of a dog, its calls are generally quite shrill. Its hunting skills are well adapted to its environment. In some areas, for example, the golden eagle will snatch up a tortoise and drop it from a great height in order to smash its shell before eating it. In other areas, golden eagles may prey on cats. They prefer to capture their quarry on the ground, swooping down low, rather than catching birds in the air.

IDENTIFICATION

- Brown overall, with yellowish-brown plumage restricted to the back of the head, and also extending down the nape of the neck.

- Long wings; well-spread primary feathers.

- Large, hooked bill has yellow base and dark tip.

- Feet are yellow with long black talons.

- Thick legs.

- Females bigger than males.

The golden eagle's tail is broad and square at the tip.

FACT FILE

Distribution Sporadic throughout the Mediterranean area into Asia. Present in Scotland, Scandinavia and eastwards into Asia. Also occurs in North Africa

Size 90cm/35in

Habitat Mountainous regions

Nest Massive cliff nest made of sticks

Eggs 2, white with dark markings

Food Mainly birds and mammals

Griffon Vulture

Eurasian vulture *Gyps fulvus*

These vultures glide over plains, using their keen eyesight to help them locate carcasses on the ground below. Rising currents of warm air, known as thermals, enable them to soar and remain airborne with little effort. Groups of vultures may be encountered scavenging at rubbish dumps. Griffon vultures nest in colonies that have been known to contain as many as 150 pairs. Chicks develop slowly, often not embarking on their first flight until they are nearly 20 weeks old. Young birds are unlikely to breed until they are at least four years old.

IDENTIFICATION

- Dark brown area around the eyes; top of the head and neck whitish.
- Light brown body, back and wings, darker flight feathers and tail.
- Relatively elongated horn-coloured bill that is curved on the upper tip.
- Legs and feet grey, and whitish on the inner thighs.
- Sexes are alike.
- Young birds have a darker brown back and also a brown neck collar.

Well-spread primary feathers enable the vulture to adjust its movements in the air.

FACT FILE

Distribution The Iberian Peninsula and western North Africa, east into the Middle East and Asia. Young birds may migrate further south into western and eastern parts of Africa
Size 110cm/43in
Habitat Mountain country
Nest Sticks located on rocky crags
Eggs 1, white with reddish-brown markings
Food Carrion

Imperial Eagle

Eastern imperial eagle *Aquila heliaca*

The population of imperial eagles declined dramatically during the 1900s, but now they are protected, their numbers are increasing. In countries such as Hungary they can be seen in open countryside, rather than retreating to the safety of mountain forests, away from human persecution. Imperial eagles, like others of their kind, are potentially long-lived birds, having few natural enemies apart from people. Young birds may not breed for the first time until they are six years old, when they are still likely to be in immature plumage.

IDENTIFICATION

- Mainly dark brown, with a paler buff area at the back of the head and around the neck. Patches of white in the shoulder area.
- The bill is yellow with a dark tip. Feet are yellow.
- Sexes are alike.

The tail has distinctive pale patches.

FACT FILE

Distribution Eastern Europe into Turkey and east across much of central Asia. Migrates south to eastern Africa and parts of Asia, including the Middle East, for winter
Size 84cm/33in
Habitat Prefers areas of open country
Nest Made of sticks and other vegetation
Eggs 2, white with dark markings
Food Small mammals, birds and carrion

Sparrowhawk

Eurasian sparrowhawk *Accipiter nisus*

This bird of prey hunts mainly birds that feed on the ground. The male sparrowhawk is smaller than the female and therefore tends to take smaller quarry. Even the females rarely take birds much bigger than pigeons, and also prey on smaller birds such as thrushes. Sparrowhawks nest later in the year than many songbirds, so that they can prey on nestlings more easily to feed their own chicks. Their short wings mean that sparrowhawks are very agile in flight, able to manoeuvre easily in wooded areas. They approach quietly with the aim of catching their target unawares, and seize hold of prey using their powerful feet.

The reddish areas stretching down from the sides of the face mark the male birds out from the females.

The sharp, hooked bill is small, but very effective for tearing flesh.

The sparrowhawk's long tail acts like a rudder to help it manoeuvre in the air as it flies.

IDENTIFICATION

- Grey head, back and wings with darker barring on the grey tail.
- The underparts are barred.
- Has bare yellow legs and feet with fairly long toes.
- Male birds are smaller than females and have pale rufous areas on the lower sides of the face that extend to the chest. In addition, the barring on their underparts is browner.

▲ *Young male sparrowhawks fledge several days before the heavier females.*

FACT FILE

Distribution Resident throughout most of Europe (except the far north of Scandinavia), North Africa and the Canary Islands. Migratory birds overwinter around the Red Sea. Distribution also extends east to Asia

Size 28cm/11in

Habitat Lightly wooded areas; now found in towns

Nest Made of sticks in a tree or on some buildings

Eggs 4–6, pale blue with reddish-brown markings

Food Mainly birds

Red Kite

Milvus milvus

When seeking prey, the red kite's unequalled flying ability allows it to hover effortlessly for hours, relying on its keen eyesight to spot movement down on the ground. It then drops and sweeps low to home in on the target. Although they are agile hunters, red kites also seek out carrion, such as dead sheep. This led farmers to fear that they were killing lambs and their numbers were reduced by putting poison in the carcasses they fed on. In recent years, thanks to the efforts of conservationists, the Welsh population of red kites has increased each year.

The white area under the wings is seen clearly in flight.

IDENTIFICATION

- Reddish brown, with a greyish head streaked with darker markings. Darker mottling over the wings. Streaking on the underparts.
- White areas under the wings and forked tail.
- Feet are yellowish with black talons.
- Sexes are alike.

FACT FILE

Distribution Wales, Iberian Peninsula and the adjacent area of North Africa. Extends north-east across Europe to southern Sweden and into the Caucasus

Size 66cm/26in

Habitat Lightly wooded regions

Nest Platform made of sticks in a tree

Eggs 1–4, white with reddish-brown markings

Food Small birds, mammals and carrion

Hen Harrier

Northern harrier *Circus cyaneus*

When hunting, hen harriers fly low over moorland, seeking not just small mammals but also birds such as grouse, which has led to their persecution by gamekeepers. Over the winter, however, they may be forced to feed largely on carrion. Their range extends into tundra areas, but they head south before winter begins. Unusually, they not only frequently roost but also breed on the ground. After the breeding season, they may gather at communal sites, which are used for several generations.

The large eyes and strong, hooked beak are typical of hunting birds.

IDENTIFICATION

- Mainly chestnut streaked with white. Darker over the wings.
- Narrow white band around eye, with solid brown area beneath.
- Barred tail, dark bill and yellow legs. White rump.
- Females are larger.

FACT FILE

Distribution Throughout much of the northern hemisphere. Extends across most of Europe, including Scandinavia, east to Asia. Often moves south for the winter as far as North Africa

Size 52cm/20in

Habitat Moorland

Nest On the ground, hidden in vegetation

Eggs 3–5, whitish

Food Small mammals and birds

Peregrine Falcon

Falco peregrinus

A powerful and skilful hunter, the peregrine falcon can swoop down on other birds at great speed. Indeed, it is thought that it can dive as quickly as 350kmh/217mph. Pigeons are a favourite prey, and peregrines may also hunt waterfowl. The impact made by their feet when they strike in the air is so great that their quarry is frequently killed instantaneously. These falcons are highly adaptable and can occasionally be sighted in cities, where apartment blocks replace the crags from which they would normally fly on hunting excursions.

BIRDWATCH

The peregrine falcon can be recognized by its bullet-shaped body and broad, pointed wings. The best time to see a peregrine is during the nesting season on ledges, crags or sea cliffs. Watch for birds winging overhead or soaring in circles. During the winter months, the peregine may move to a lowland hunting ground, such as an estuary, where it can sometimes be seen resting on the ground.

▼*Plunging down from a great height in a dramatic "stoop", the peregrine catches many of its victims in the air.*

The peregrine has acute eyesight and can spot prey from a height of 300m/1,000ft.

FACT FILE

IDENTIFICATION

- Dark grey upperparts.
- A broad blackish stripe extends down below the eyes; the surrounding white area extends right around the throat.
- The barring on the chest is lighter than on the abdomen.
- Darker markings are apparent on the grey feathers of the back and wings.
- The tail is barred with paler grey feathering at the base.
- The legs and feet are yellow.
- Relatively narrow wings when seen in flight.
- Females are much larger than males.

Distribution Resident throughout most of western Europe and much of Africa, apart from the Sahara Desert and the central rainforest band. One of the most adaptable and widely distributed birds of prey, occurring on all continents

Size 38–51cm/15–20in

Habitat Usually near cliffs, and sometimes open ground

Nest Usually on cliff ledges

Eggs 3–4, whitish with red-brown markings

Food Birds

Merlin

Pigeon hawk *Falco columbarius*

These highly adaptable hawks can be seen in a wide range of environments. They tend to breed in the far north where there is little cover, swooping low and fast above the ground in search of prey. Pairs may hunt for quarry together, increasing their chances of making a kill. Merlins have even been seen hunting along with other birds of prey. The merlin prefers to tackle birds in flight rather than seizing them when they are perching.

IDENTIFICATION

- Orange-brown underparts with dark streaks. Crown and wings are blue-grey with dark streaks. White cheeks with dark streaks.
- Broad dark band on the tail-tip.
- Females have brown-grey upperparts and four or five light bands on the tail.
- Males usually smaller than females.

The merlin rests in a totally upright position as it surveys the countryside.

FACT FILE

Distribution Present in the British Isles throughout the year. Occurs in Scandinavia, moving south in the winter down to North Africa. Occurs in Asia and the Americas also
Size 33cm/13in
Habitat Lightly wooded and open countryside
Nest In trees or sometimes on the ground
Eggs 3–6, buff with variable reddish speckling
Food Mostly birds

Kestrel

Common kestrel *Falco tinnunculus*

These birds of prey are often seen hovering over busy roads, where they catch prey on the roadside as traffic passes by. The kestrel's keen eyesight enables it to spot quarry as small as grasshoppers on the ground. In the winter, kestrels hunt earthworms drawn to the surface by heavy rainfall. They will also venture into towns, where they hunt in parks.

The kestrel is instantly recognizable as it hovers. It appears totally still, with head down and wings raised.

IDENTIFICATION

- Bluish-grey head, black stripe under the eyes and whitish throat. Wings chestnut brown with black markings.
- Black spots on pale brown chest and abdomen.
- Rump and tail feathers grey with black tips.
- Females are similar to males, but have browner heads and distinct barring across the tail feathers.

FACT FILE

Distribution Throughout western Europe to southern Asia and North Africa. Also breeds in Scandinavia
Size 37cm/14.5in
Habitat Open countryside
Nest Platform made of sticks in a tree or in farm buildings
Eggs 3–7, pale pink with dark brown markings
Food Invertebrates and small mammals

Gyr Falcon

Falco rusticolus

The largest of the falcons, the gyr falcon is well adapted to surviving in the far north, where its colouring helps to conceal its presence, even in areas where there is little tree cover. These falcons are often sighted in coastal regions, where they prey on seabirds. They fly quite low when hunting in open countryside, taking grouse and similar birds as well as small rodents, and prefer to catch their quarry on the ground rather than in flight. When breeding, pairs may even adopt artificial sites, nesting in buildings associated with oil pipelines, for example.

The white form of the gyr falcon is almost entirely white with dark flecks.

FACT FILE

Distribution Iceland and Scandinavia. Found as an annual vagrant in the British Isles
Size 63cm/25in
Habitat Mainly taiga and tundra
Nest On cliff ledges
Eggs 3–4, buff with dense reddish speckling
Food Small birds and mammals

IDENTIFICATION

■ Variable in colour. Typically blue-grey with barring across the back, wings and tail. Dark areas at the side of the face. Whitish underparts with dark bars.

■ There is a white form that is found mainly in Greenland, a light grey form found in Iceland, and a dark grey form that occurs in Scandinavia and northern Russia.

Common Buzzard

Eurasian buzzard *Buteo buteo*

With its rather stocky, broad shape, the buzzard is fairly easy to identify in flight. It soars and glides over large areas before suddenly swooping down to seize a small mammal such as a rabbit – its traditional prey, particularly in Europe. Buzzards also hunt invertebrates, methodically searching the ground in pursuit of their quarry. They may even be spotted on roads on occasion, feeding on road kill, sometimes placing themselves in danger from passing traffic. The buzzard is one of the most common birds of prey in Europe because of its adaptability to changing habitats and food supplies.

Most buzzards are brown, though there is a rare white form.

FACT FILE

Distribution Resident in western Europe. Summer resident in parts of Scandinavia and east across Asia. European migratory birds overwinter in certain parts of southern and eastern Africa
Size 57cm/22in
Habitat Areas with trees
Nest Platform made of sticks, usually in a tree
Eggs 2–4, white
Food Small mammals and other prey

IDENTIFICATION

■ Mainly dark brown. A variable amount of white plumage around the bill and on the underparts.

■ Tail is barred with paler plumage at the top.

■ Legs and feet are yellow and the bill is yellow with a dark tip.

■ Females are often larger than males.

Common Pheasant

Ring-necked pheasant *Phasianus colchicus*

The pheasant's natural range is in Asia, but they have been bred in Europe and released into the wild for shooting. It is one of the most popular game birds. Breeding has resulted in a considerable variation in the appearance of individual birds. Pheasants usually live in groups made up of a cock bird with several hens. The cock pheasant is brilliantly coloured, with a long, elegant tail. The hens are a dull mottled brown, which helps to camouflage them when they are sitting on their eggs on the ground. Pheasants forage for food on the ground, although they fly noisily and somewhat clumsily when disturbed and may also choose to roost off the ground.

The ear tufts may be very prominent.

The areas of red skin on either side of the cock pheasant's face are one of its main distinguishing features.

The pheasant's tail feathers are long and very elegant.

Some races have a white ring around the neck.

The cock, or ▶ male pheasant.

FACT FILE

IDENTIFICATION

- Prominent areas of bare red skin feature on each side of the face. They are surrounded by dark greenish, metallic plumage.

- Has a variable white area of plumage at the base of the neck.

- The remainder of the plumage is brown, with the underparts a more chestnut shade with dark blotching apparent.

- Females are lighter brown overall, with darker mottling, especially on the back and the wings.

The hen pheasant is smaller than the cock and dull brown in colour.

▲ *The hen, or female common pheasant.*

Distribution Now present throughout most of western Europe, apart from much of the Iberian Peninsula. Occurs in a band in central Asia as far east as Japan, and has also been introduced to the United States, Tasmania, Australia and New Zealand

Size Cock 89cm/35in; hen 62cm/24in

Habitat Lightly wooded regions

Nest Scrape on the ground

Eggs 7–15, olive brown

Food Plant matter, such as seeds, berries and young shoots, and invertebrates

Red-legged Partridge

Alectoris rufa

The red-legged partridge is an adaptable bird and is now breeding well outside its natural range. It was first brought to England for sporting purposes as long ago as the late 1600s. During the 20th century the chukar partridge, which is similar in appearance to the red-legged variety, was introduced to the British Isles. Today it can be difficult to tell whether a particular bird is a pure or cross-bred red-legged partridge. During the autumn and winter red-legged partridges gather in large groups and feed together, on fairly open ground or in scrub. The flock breaks up in the spring to form breeding pairs that remain together through the summer. The cock bird chooses, then prepares, the nest site.

Male birds have a tarsal spur on the legs.

The black collar and dark streaking around the neck are major identification features.

IDENTIFICATION

- Dark necklace; streaks around the neck.
- Black stripe extends across the eye with narrow white band above and white area extending down the throat.
- Bluish-grey coloration above the bill and on the breast and barred flanks. Brownish abdomen.
- Females are smaller, with no tarsal spur.

FACT FILE

Distribution Found naturally in Europe from the Iberian Peninsula to Italy. Introduced to the rest of Europe

Size 38cm/15in

Habitat Open countryside

Nest Scrape on the ground

Eggs 9–12, pale yellowish brown with dark spotting

Food Plant matter and some invertebrates

Rock Partridge

Alectoris graeca

The name of these partridges reflects the fact that they are often observed on rocky slopes, which in Italy are sometimes as high as 2,700m/8,850ft. They move down to lower levels when snow collects on the slopes in winter. Throughout the year, rock partridges are rarely found very far from water, and they are most likely to be observed in flocks. Their colouring provides excellent camouflage when they are on the ground. When flushed (disturbed), their flight is quite low and fast, and they will dip down into nearby cover again as soon as they are out of apparent danger. Rock partridges nest as individual pairs, and their chicks are fully grown by three months old.

A very distinct black band separates the white throat from the grey breast.

IDENTIFICATION

- Grey crown. Black stripe runs from around red bill across the eye and on to the chest, bordering a white throat.
- Underparts are greyish-blue, becoming fawn, with black-and-white barring on the flanks. Brownish on back.
- Sexes are alike.

FACT FILE

Distribution Central southern Europe, from France east to Italy, Sicily, Greece and the former Yugoslavia.

Size 36cm/14in

Habitat Rocky alpine regions

Nest Scrape on the ground

Eggs 8–14, yellowish brown with some darker spotting

Food Plant matter and some invertebrates

Capercaillie

Western capercaillie *Tetrao urogallus*

The male capercaillie is similar in size to a turkey. Because of its large size and tasty flesh, it has been widely hunted by humans. It became extinct in Great Britain in the 18th century, but has been reintroduced to the conifer forests of Scotland. The female is much smaller than the male bird. After mating with her chosen partner, the hen nests and rears the young by herself. The weather in the critical post-hatching period has a major impact on the survival rate of the chicks. Both sexes have strong, hooked bills, which enable them to nip off pieces of tough vegetation, such as Scots pine shoots, with ease, allowing them to survive even when snow covers the ground.

When displaying, the cock fans its tail feathers.

The females are about a third the weight of the males.

The bluish green sheen on the chest is highly distinctive.

IDENTIFICATION

- Greyish-black head with a red stripe above each eye. Shaggy "beard" of loose feathers.
- Green area on the chest, with chestnut wings.
- Rump and tail are blackish.
- Underparts are variable, ranging from predominantly white to black.
- Legs are covered with brown feathers, and toes are exposed.
- Females have an orangish patch on the sides of the face and chest, brown mottled upperparts and whiter underparts.

BIRDWATCH

The male capercaillie has an elaborate courtship ritual. Each dawn, males go to the display ground. They spread their tail and neck ruff and drag their wings on the ground. At intervals the birds leap up, thrashing the air with their wings to make a rushing sound.

FACT FILE

Distribution Scotland and mountainous parts of western Europe. Also ranges through large areas of Scandinavia and northern Asia

Size 80–115cm/ 31–45in

Habitat Areas with coniferous and deciduous trees

Nest Shallow scrape on the ground

Eggs 6–10, yellow with light brown blotches

Food Mainly buds and shoots

Swift

Common swift *Apus apus*

Flocks of swifts are most likely to be spotted when they are uttering their distinctive screaming calls, flying low overhead in search of winged insects. At other times, they may be seen as little more than distant specks, wheeling at heights of more than 1,000m/3,300ft. Their flight pattern is quite distinctive, consisting of a series of rapid wingbeats followed by gliding into the wind. The structure of their feet does not allow them to perch, although they can cling to vertical surfaces. If hunting conditions are unfavourable, such as a cool summer, nestling swifts respond by growing more slowly, while adults can remain dormant for short periods to avoid starvation.

◀ *Swifts spend their time in the air when they are not breeding.*

The swift's forked tail is very short.

IDENTIFICATION

- Dark overall, with pointed wing tips and a forked tail.
- Pale whitish-coloured throat area.
- Sexes are alike.

FACT FILE

Distribution Found virtually across the whole of Europe, also extending to North Africa and Asia. Overwinters in southern Africa

Size 16.5cm/6.5in

Habitat In the air

Nest Cup-shaped structure under cover

Eggs 2–3, white

Food Flying invertebrates, such as midges and moths

Red-backed Shrike

Lanius collurio

Like many insectivorous birds, the red-backed shrike migrates south to Africa each autumn, spending the winter in savanna areas, where food is more plentiful. In some parts of this shrike's breeding range, its nests are targeted by the cuckoo. Unlike many host species, however, pairs learn to recognize cuckoo eggs laid alongside their own and discard them from the nest. Cock birds impale their prey on the sharp spines of plants during the breeding season, as this ensures a more constant supply of food for their chicks.

The male's black eye stripe extends back from the bill.

IDENTIFICATION

- Male has light grey crown with black stripe across the eyes. Pinkish underparts with reddish-brown back and wings.
- Female has brownish area at the front of the crown, grey behind and dark brown wings. Underparts are white with darker edging to the feathers. Brown patches behind the eyes.

FACT FILE

Distribution Mainland Europe, except for most of the Iberian Peninsula and northern parts of Scandinavia. Extends into Asia, and also overwinters in Africa, south of the Equator

Size 18cm/7in

Habitat Open country

Nest Cup-shaped, in the fork of a bush or tree

Eggs 5–9, variable coloration

Food Invertebrates

Common Skylark

Alauda arvensis

The colouring of the skylark enables it to remain hidden on the ground, where it sometimes freezes to escape detection. If disturbed at close quarters, it takes off almost vertically. Skylarks are unusual in that they reveal their presence readily by singing. They engage in what are described as song flights – fluttering their wings, they rise slowly through the air to a height of 100m/330ft or so. The female skylark builds a nest in a hollow in the ground. Two or three clutches of eggs are laid during late spring and early summer. During the breeding period, a sitting hen may draw attention away from her nest site by pretending to be injured, dragging one wing along the ground and taking off only as a last resort.

◀ *The skylark is famous for its powerful and clear song.*

The skylark can be told from a song thrush by its smaller size.

The longish tail has white outer feathers.

The eggs are grey-white, spotted with brown.

◀ *The skylark's nest is well concealed on the grassy ground.*

FACT FILE

Distribution Resident throughout much of western Europe from Denmark southwards. Also occurs in North Africa. Breeding range extends further north to Scandinavia and eastwards to Asia

Size 18cm/7in

Habitat Open countryside, especially farmland

Nest On the ground, hidden in grass

Eggs 3–5, greyish, with dark spots

Food Plant matter and invertebrates

IDENTIFICATION

- Greyish-brown plumage over the back and wings, with speckling becoming paler on the flanks.
- Underparts are mainly white.
- Whitish stripe extends back from the eyes, and the ear coverts are greyish.
- Short crest on the crown, although it is not always visible.
- Females are similar to males but lack the crest.

BIRDWATCH

The male skylark's display flight is accompanied by a chirruping song that lasts for up to five minutes. This helps to pinpoint the bird, even when it is just a speck in the sky. The skylark also sings on the ground, but if it is disturbed, it will instantly rise up into the air, singing loudly. This bird sings almost all year round, except when the female is nest-building and sitting on eggs.

Hoopoe

Eurasian hoopoe Upupa epops

The "hoo, hoo" sound of its call gives this bird its common name. The hoopoe perches and roosts high up in trees or on rooftops. It feeds mainly on the ground, using its long bill to probe for insects or larvae, or to grab prey such as lizards scurrying through the grass. The male attracts a mate by bowing to a female and nodding the large crest up and down. Hoopoes are not especially shy of people, and pairs sometimes nest in buildings. They may often be observed dust-bathing, which keeps their plumage in good condition. Hoopoes leave their breeding sites in August or September to overwinter in Africa, returning in April when temperatures begin to rise.

The large, black-edged crest is usually held flat unless the hoopoe is excited.

The long, slender bill is ideal for probing the ground for grubs and insects.

The bold black and white stripes on the wings are very distinctive.

The square-shaped tail has a broad white band.

FACT FILE

Distribution Throughout most of Europe, although usually absent from Scandinavia and the British Isles. Overwinters in Africa south of the Equator. Also occurs in parts of North Africa and much of central Africa

Size 29cm/11in

Habitat Relatively open country

Nest In secluded holes

Eggs 5–8, whitish to yellowish olive

Food Mainly invertebrates, and especially worms

IDENTIFICATION

- Mainly pale buff, although more orange on the crown and with black edging to the feathers.

- Alternate bands of black-and-white colouring on the wings.

- Long, narrow bill curves downwards.

- Sexes are alike.

BIRDWATCH

The hoopoe's unusual appearance often helps to identify it, especially as it is most likely to be seen in open country. When in flight, the broad shape of the wings is clearly visible. The crest is held flat over the back of the head, though it is often raised when the bird lands.

Bee-eater

European bee-eater *Merops apiaster*

The bill is longish, and slightly curved.

In spite of their name, European bee-eaters hawk a much wider range of prey in the air than simply bees. More than 300 different invertebrates have been identified in their diet, ranging from dragonflies to butterflies. They have even been known to swoop on spiders, seizing them from their webs. Although individual birds go hunting on their own, European bee-eaters nest in colonies of up to eight pairs. Sandy cliffs, where they can excavate their breeding tunnels with relative ease, are favoured nesting sites. Outside the breeding season, groups roost huddled together on branches.

Coloration and patterning on the head is a good spotting feature.

The long tail is shiny above, and duller below.

The bright plumage includes green, blue, yellow, chestnut brown and gold feathers.

The central feathers are longer than the other tail feathers.

IDENTIFICATION

- Whitish band above the black bill, merging into blue above the eyes.
- Chestnut brown extends from the top of the head down over the back, and across the wings.
- Golden shoulders and rump.
- Black band extends from the bill across the eyes.
- Throat is yellow, with a black band separating this area from bluish underparts.
- Females have more green on wings and shoulders.

BIRDWATCH

The bee-eater is one of the most brightly coloured European birds and because of this is usually easy to recognize as it perches on a branch or telegraph wire waiting for prey. In addition to its striking body and wing coloration, the bee-eater also has a highly distinctive tail, with a pair of central feathers that are longer than the other feathers.

FACT FILE

Distribution Much of southern Europe, extending into adjacent parts of Asia and into North Africa. Overwinters in western and southern parts of Africa
Size 25cm/10in
Habitat Open country
Nest Tunnel in bank or cliff
Eggs 4–10, white
Food Mainly flying invertebrates

Pied Flycatcher

Ficedula hypoleuca

These flycatchers hawk invertebrates in flight, as well as catching slower-moving prey such as caterpillars by plucking them off vegetation. They are frequently seen in oak woodlands in Europe during the summer, but may range north to the taiga. Here, mosquitoes hatching in pools of water during the brief summer provide an almost constant food supply. Pied flycatchers are closely related to collared flycatchers and sometimes mate with them. However, the male collared flycatcher has a conspicuous white collar to distinguish it, and the females are greyer in colour.

In the breeding season the male pied flycatcher has striking black and white plumage.

Distinctive white wing panel.

The male has a white forehead in both winter and summer plumage.

The underparts are totally white.

IDENTIFICATION

- Plumage in summer is a combination of black and white, with white patches above the bill and on the wings.

- Underparts are white while the remainder of the plumage is black.

- Hens also have whitish underparts, with a white area on the wing, while the upperparts are brownish.

- Males during winter resemble females, but retain blackish wing and uppertail coverts.

BIRDWATCH

During the breeding season the male pied flycatcher is strikingly black and white. In winter the male bird is not so easy to recognize as the plumage is greyish-brown like the females, although the forehead remains white. Flycatchers with a narrow black area on the nape of the neck are male offspring from a cross between a pied and a collared flycatcher.

FACT FILE

Distribution Summer visitor to Europe, breeding as far north as Scandinavia. Overwinters in Africa

Size 13cm/5in

Habitat Areas in which insects are common

Nest Hole in a tree

Eggs 5–9, pale blue

Food Invertebrates

Grey Wagtail

Motacilla cinerea

Darker feathering disappears from the throat in winter.

Fast-flowing streams are where grey wagtails are most likely to be observed, as they dart fearlessly across rocks in search of invertebrates. They live in pairs and construct their cup-shaped nests in well-hidden spots, among the roots of a tree or on an ivy-clad wall, and usually close to water. Grey wagtails have benefited from some changes in their environment, taking advantage of millstreams and adjacent buildings to expand their area of distribution, but they can still be forced to leave their usual territory in search of food during severe winters, especially if the water freezes.

IDENTIFICATION

- Grey head and wings. Narrow white band with black beneath runs across the eyes.
- White border to black bib on the throat.
- Underparts are yellow – brightest on the chest and at the base of the long tail.
- Sexes are similar but females have a grey bib and much whiter underparts.

FACT FILE

Distribution Resident throughout most of western Europe, except Scandinavia. Also present in North Africa and Asia, where the population tends to be more migratory

Size 20cm/8in

Habitat Near to flowing water

Nest In rock crevices and similar sites

Eggs 4–6, buff with greyish, marbled markings

Food Invertebrates

Pied Wagtail

Motacilla alba

◀ *Coloration varies across the pied wagtail's range.*

These lively birds have adapted to changes in their environment, moving from coastal areas and marshland into farmland. Today they can often be observed hunting on and beside roads. Pied wagtails are not especially shy birds, and the movements of their tail feathers, which give them their common name, strike an unmistakable jaunty pose. The pied wagtail that breeds in the British Isles is different from those found elsewhere in Europe: males in Britain have black plumage on their backs during the summer. This turns to grey for the rest of the year. The mainland Europe pied wagtail is often described as the white wagtail, as it has a greyish back for the whole year.

IDENTIFICATION

- Variable through range. Prominent white area on the head. Black crown and nape.
- Black area extends from throat down on to chest. Rest of underparts white.
- Back is grey or black.
- Females have more ashy grey backs, which form a smudged border with the black feathering above.

FACT FILE

Distribution Resident throughout western Europe and in western North Africa, with the winter distribution there more widespread. Seen in Scandinavia and Iceland only during the summer months

Size 19cm/7.5in

Habitat Open areas

Nest Concealed, sometimes in walls

Eggs 5–6, whitish with grey markings

Food Invertebrates

Rock Ptarmigan

Lagopus mutus

The rock ptarmigan is the member of the grouse family best adapted to the cold regions of the far north. It gets its name from a capacity to survive in barren, rocky areas of the Arctic. When snow is on the ground, the ptarmigan feeds on buds and twigs of shrubs such as willow, which manage to grow in this treeless region. At breeding time, the male attracts a female with a display flight and a ground display. Pairs choose a nest site protected by shrubs. The cock stays nearby while the hen incubates alone. The chicks are covered in down when they hatch and can move easily, but are not able to fly until their flight feathers have emerged fully, at about ten days old.

◀ *These male birds are at different stages of shedding their winter plumage.*

Summer plumage is mottled brown, which acts as a camouflage against the vegetation.

Winter plumage is white, with a black edge to the tail.

FACT FILE

IDENTIFICATION

- Mottled, brownish head with red above the eyes.
- Similar patterning across the body in summer, becoming white in winter.
- Blackish stripes on the face, lacking in females.

BIRDWATCH

The rock ptarmigan's plumage changes radically during the course of each year. Its white winter feathers "disappear" against the snow on the ground. Then, when the snow melts, the ptarmigan's lower parts stay white, but its back turns grey-brown, merging with the rock of the surrounding landscape.

Distribution Favours mountainous areas. Found in Iceland, northern Scandinavia, the Scottish Highlands, the Alpine region and the Pyrenees mountains between France and Spain

Size 38cm/15in

Habitat Tundra

Nest Scrape on the ground lined with vegetation

Eggs 6–9, creamy buff, heavily blotched with blackish brown spots

Food Berries, buds and leaves

Common Quail

Eurasian migratory quail *Coturnix coturnix*

These small quails often inhabit agricultural areas. They are shy birds and are hard to spot because of the effective camouflage provided by their plumage. Common quails prefer to remain concealed, but take to the wing when necessary, when they are both agile and fast. Their wings appear quite large when flying, reflecting the fact that these small birds fly long distances each year to spend the winter in Africa. The resident African population of common quails are not quite the same as the migratory birds, being slightly smaller in size. They are also more reddish-brown in their colouring. Throughout their range, common quails prefer areas of grassland, as this vegetation provides them with natural cover.

The coloration on the face and throat is a good spotting feature.

IDENTIFICATION

- A pale stripe above the eye. A thinner, narrower black stripe runs beneath. Small white area faintly bordered by black on upper chest.
- Top of head and back dark brown.
- The rest of the underparts are fawn, becoming paler on the abdomen.
- Females lack the white patch, have mottled plumage and are duller.

FACT FILE

Distribution Occurs in Europe in summer, wintering in Africa south of the Sahara. Also resident in North Africa
Size 18cm/7in
Habitat Open country
Nest Grass-lined scrape on the ground
Eggs 5–13, buff with darker markings
Food Seeds and some invertebrates

Great Bustard

Otis tarda

These massive birds have declined in number because of hunting and habitat change. They still flourish in undisturbed areas, where they are seen in groups throughout the year. The courtship display of the cock is an amazing sight as he bends forwards, raising his wings and inflating his throat sac. His head disappears from view as he appears to turn himself inside out. Despite their size, great bustards are quiet birds by nature, uttering a short call resembling a bark only if alarmed. Although adults will hunt voles, the chicks are reared on insects and then plant food. By five weeks the chicks can fly and search for food themselves, but they are not independent until about a year old.

The upturned tail makes this bird look even larger than it is.

FACT FILE

IDENTIFICATION

- Grey head and neck, with a reddish area at base. Chestnut and black wing markings, with white areas. Underparts and tail tips white.
- Hens have more extensive but paler red colouring on the neck, and less white on the wings.

Distribution Scattered throughout the Iberian Peninsula. Also present in parts of central Europe and ranges eastwards into Asia
Size Cock 105cm/41in; hen 75cm/29.5in
Habitat Open steppes and farmland
Nest Flattened area of vegetation
Eggs 2–4, greenish or olive brown
Food Plant matter, invertebrates and small mammals

81

City and Garden

Bird tables and feeders help to attract birds into our gardens by providing them with additional food sources. For birds that are resident throughout the year, these are especially welcome during cold winter weather. Pigeons and doves have adapted well to living in cities, using buildings as nesting sites, although their presence is not always welcomed.

Common Blackbird

Turdus merula

The blackbird is a familiar sight in town, city and country gardens, where it can often be seen looking for invertebrates on lawns. After rain, earthworms, the blackbird's favourite food, are drawn to the surface, and slugs and snails also emerge in wet conditions. In the 19th century blackbirds were rarely seen in gardens, but today they are common.
The blackbird is very vocal, uttering a variety of calls. The male is renowned for its beautiful song, and both sexes will utter an urgent, harsh alarm call. Although blackbirds do not associate together in flocks, pairs sometimes forage together. As with other members of the thrush family, their tails are very flexible and can be raised or lowered at will. It is not unusual to see pied blackbirds, with variable amounts of white feathering among the black plumage. Most of these birds, especially those with extensive white areas, are males.

The blackbird's eyes have a yellow ring around them.

The male's glossy black plumage lives up to the bird's name – unlike the female.

IDENTIFICATION

- Plumage is a magnificent jet black, contrasting with the bright yellow bill, which becomes a deeper shade during the winter.

- Females are drab in comparison – brownish overall with some streaks, notably on the breast, and with a darker bill.

▼ *The hen alone incubates the eggs, which hatch after 12 to 14 days.*

FACT FILE

Distribution Resident throughout most of Europe and North Africa. The majority of Scandinavian and eastern European populations are migratory

Size 29cm/11.5in

Habitat Woodland, gardens and parkland

Nest Well-hidden cup-shaped nest

Eggs 3–5, greenish blue with reddish-brown markings

Food Invertebrates, fruit and berries

Song Thrush

Turdus philomelos

The lovely song of these thrushes is particularly noticeable in spring, at the start of the breeding season, and it is usually delivered from a relatively high branch. Song thrushes are welcomed by gardeners because they eat snails and other garden pests. Having grabbed a snail, the song thrush chooses a hard surface such as a stone, called an anvil, and then batters the snail against this anvil to break the shell and dislodge the mollusc inside. Song thrushes run along the ground to pursue quarry such as leather-jackets (the larvae of certain species of cranefly). When breeding, the hen is mainly, or even solely, responsible for building the cup-shaped nest.

The bill shape is adapted to a diet of earthworms and other invertebrates.

Look for arrow-shaped markings here.

IDENTIFICATION

- Has brown back and wings, with some black areas, and also a yellow-buff area across the chest. Dark arrow-shaped markings over the chest and abdomen.

- Sexes are alike.

FACT FILE

Distribution Ranges widely throughout Europe. Eastern populations head south to the Mediterranean region for the winter. Also in North Africa, even as far south as the Sudan

Size 22cm/8.5in

Habitat Woodlands and gardens

Nest Cup-shaped

Eggs 5–6, greenish blue with reddish-brown markings

Food Invertebrates and berries

Robin

Erithacus rubecula

The robin is perhaps the best known of all British birds. It is a common visitor to gardens. Once attracted to food put out on a bird table, it will return to it all winter long. A robin can become very tame, hopping down alongside the gardener's fork to grab worms and other invertebrates as they come to the surface. It is a highly territorial bird, defending its patch very aggressively. If alarmed by a predator, such as a cat, the robin makes a long, drawn-out, "tic-tic" call. Young robins look different from mature birds – they are almost entirely brown with dense spotting on the head and chest.

The red breast is the robin's most important spotting feature.

IDENTIFICATION

- Bright orange plumage extends just above the bill, around the eyes and down over virtually the entire breast.

- Lower underparts are whitish grey, becoming browner on the flanks.

- Top of the head and wings are brown, with a pale wing bar.

- Sexes are alike.

FACT FILE

Distribution Resident in the British Isles, western Europe and also parts of North Africa. Scandinavian and eastern European populations are migratory, overwintering further south

Size 14cm/5.5in

Habitat Gardens, parks and woodland areas

Nest Under cover, often near the ground

Eggs 5–7, bluish white with red markings

Food Invertebrates, berries, fruit and seeds

Feral Pigeon

Rock dove *Columba livia*

Although true rock doves have a localized range, their descendants – feral pigeons – are a very common sight even in very large cities. In the past, monastic communities kept and bred rock doves, and the young doves, known as squabs, were highly valued as a source of meat. Inevitably, some birds escaped from their dovecotes, and the offspring of these birds, which reverted to the wild, gave rise to today's populations of feral pigeons. Colour mutations (changes in coloration) have also occurred. Apart from the so-called "blue" form, there are now red and even mainly white individuals on city streets today, scavenging whatever they can from our leftovers.

Green iridescent feathers on the neck are a distinguishing feature.

▼ *The feral pigeon is one of Europe's best-known and most-spotted birds, now found in large numbers in our towns and cities.*

The black wing bars are more obvious when the bird is flying.

Feral pigeons often have longer wings than doves.

IDENTIFICATION

- Dark bluish-grey head, and a slight green iridescence on the neck.

- Light grey wings and two characteristic black bars across each wing.

- Reddish-purple colouring on each side of the upper chest.

- Remainder of the plumage is grey with a black band at the tip of the tail feathers.

- Sexes are alike.

▼ *The feral pigeon nests on loose twigs.*

FACT FILE

Distribution Occurs naturally in northern areas of Scotland and nearby islands, and in western Ireland. Also found around the Mediterranean. Distribution of the feral pigeon extends throughout Europe and southern Africa, as well as to other continents

Size 35cm/14in

Habitat Originally cliffs and mountainous areas

Nest Loose pile of twigs or similar material

Eggs 2, white

Food Mainly seeds

Wood Pigeon

Columba palumbus

The wood pigeon is the largest European pigeon, easily identified by its gentle but insistent call. Farmers view it as a pest because of its fondness for seeds and grain. In towns, these birds frequent parks where there are established trees, and visit gardens and allotments to feed on crops. They also, however, eat potential pests, such as snails. Pairs sometimes nest on buildings, but prefer a suitable tree fork. Their loud calls are heard soon after dawn. Outside the breeding season, these birds congregate in larger numbers. Their relatively large size means that they appear quite clumsy when taking off.

Distinct white patches at side of neck.

The white edging to the wings is most obvious in flight.

IDENTIFICATION

- Grey head. Metallic-green area at nape of neck and white patches on the sides. Bill reddish with yellow tip.

- Purplish breast is paler on underparts.

- White wing-edges. Black tail tip.

- Sexes are alike.

FACT FILE

Distribution Occurs throughout virtually all of western Europe, and ranges eastwards into Asia. Also present in north-western Africa

Size 43cm/17in

Habitat Areas with tall trees

Nest Platform of twigs

Eggs 2, white

Food Seeds, plant matter and invertebrates

Laughing Dove

Streptopelia senegalensis

Speckled collar is a clear feature.

The highly adaptable laughing doves can often be seen in urban habitats, particularly in areas where they are expanding their range. With a constant supply of suitable food available from bird tables and feeders, they have been able to become established well away from their natural range. The doves' fast breeding cycle, with chicks hatching and leaving the nest within a month of the eggs being laid, means that they can increase their numbers rapidly under favourable conditions. Pairs may attempt to breed throughout most of the year, rather than having a fixed breeding period like many other bird species.

IDENTIFICATION

- Reddish brown. Brown and black speckled collar under the neck.

- Grey bar on the leading edge of the wing.

- Pale underparts.

- Long, relatively dark tail.

- Sexes are alike.

FACT FILE

Distribution Occur naturally across Africa, but are found in some parts of Europe, too: on the Mediterranean island of Malta and in south-eastern Turkey. It is likely that they are also spreading across other parts of Turkey

Size 26cm/10in

Habitat Acacia woodland, oases and open country

Nest Loose platform of twigs

Eggs 2, white

Food Mainly seeds and invertebrates

Collared Dove

Streptopelia decaocto

▼ *The collared dove will happily build its nest on roof-tops.*

Changes in habitat sometimes cause a particular species of bird to alter its natural range. During the second half of the 20th century, the range of the collared dove changed dramatically as it spread westwards. The reasons for this are unclear. Collared doves were recorded in Hungary in the 1930s, and they moved rapidly over the next decade across Germany and Austria to France. They also headed north to Denmark and the Netherlands. The species was first seen in eastern England during 1952, and a pair bred there three years later. The earliest Irish sighting was reported in 1959, and by the mid-1960s the collared dove had colonized almost all of the UK. No other bird species has spread naturally so far and so rapidly in recent times. The collared dove's range now extends right across Europe and Asia.

The black half-collar on the neck gives this bird its name. It also marks this bird out from other species of pigeons and doves.

The dark flight feathers have clear white edges.

FACT FILE

IDENTIFICATION

- Pale greyish-fawn with a narrow black half-collar around the back of the neck.
- Dark flight feathers with white edging along the leading edge of the wing.
- White tips to tail feathers visible when spread.
- Depth of individual colouring can vary.
- Sexes are alike.

BIRDWATCH

The many different species of doves and pigeons all belong to the same Columbiform family. They are all plump, round-bodied birds with strong legs that have four toes, and these toes are usually partly feathered. The head is small and the bill is short and rounded – an ideal shape for gathering the seeds, fruit and grain on which these birds like to feed.

Distribution Across Europe, apart from the far north of Scandinavia and the Alps, eastwards to Asia. More localized on the Iberian Peninsula and in North Africa particularly

Size 34cm/13in

Habitat Parks and gardens

Nest Platform of twigs

Eggs 2, white

Food Seeds and some plant matter

Common Nightingale

Erithacus megarhynchos

It is surprisingly difficult to spot the common nightingale. Its subdued colouring enables it to blend easily into the dense vegetation, either woodland or shrubbery, that is its preferred habitat. You can hear the nightingale's calls as dusk approaches, and even after dark on moonlit nights. The bird's large eyes indicate that this member of the thrush family is crepuscular – becoming active at dusk. The common nightingale is present in Europe from April to September, when it breeds before heading back to southern parts of Africa for winter. The nightingale repeats the journey north and its arrival is seen as heralding the start of spring.

◀ *The nightingale is famous for its beautiful, musical song.*

IDENTIFICATION

- Brown plumage extends from above the bill down over the back of the head and wings, becoming reddish brown on the rump and tail. Large dark eyes with light eye ring.

- A sandy buff area extends across the breast. Lower underparts are whitish.

- Sexes are alike.

FACT FILE

Distribution Southern England and mainland Europe on similar latitude. South into north-western Africa. Overwinters further south in Africa

Size 16cm/6in

Habitat Woodland and gardens

Nest Cup-shaped

Eggs 4–5, greyish-green to reddish-buff

Food Mainly invertebrates

House Martin

Delichon urbica

The breeding habits of the house martin have changed because of the spread of buildings in rural areas. They traditionally nest on cliffs, but over the past century they began building on the walls of houses and farm structures, as well as under bridges and even on street lamps, where a ready supply of nocturnal insects are attracted after dark. The nest is usually spherical and made of mud. The base is built first, followed by the sides, and on average the whole process takes about two weeks to complete. House martins are social by nature, occasionally nesting in huge colonies made up of thousands of pairs.

The completed nest is made up of around 2,500 beakfuls of mud.

IDENTIFICATION

- Dark bluish head and back with black wings.

- White underwing coverts, underparts and rump.

- Tail feathers are dark blue.

- Sexes are alike.

FACT FILE

Distribution Throughout Europe, overwintering in Africa south of the Sahara Desert. Also present across much of Asia

Size 13cm/5in

Habitat Open country, close to water

Nest Made of mud, cup-shaped

Eggs 4–5, white

Food Flying invertebrates

Blue Tit

Parus caeruleus

Common visitors to bird tables, blue tits are lively, active birds by nature, and are welcomed by gardeners because they eat aphids. Their small size allows them to hop up the stems of thin plants and, hanging upside down, seek these pests under leaves. Blue tits are well adapted to garden life and readily adopt nest boxes supplied for them. The young birds leave the nest before they are able to fly properly, and are vulnerable to predators such as cats at this time. Those that do survive the critical early weeks can be easily distinguished by the presence of yellow rather than white cheek patches.

Young birds have pale yellow, not white, cheek patches, and a greenish cap.

The bright blue, white-edged crown is a clear spotting feature.

Blue tits are light and acrobatic and can balance happily on very thin twigs.

The legs also have a bluish hue.

IDENTIFICATION

- Has a distinctive area of blue on the crown, edged with white, and a narrow black stripe running across the eyes.

- Cheeks are white.

- Underparts are yellowish.

- The back is a greyish-green.

- There is a whitish bar across the top of the blue wings.

- The tail is also blue.

- Sexes are similar, but females are duller.

BIRDWATCH

The blue tit's characteristic plumage of bright blue and yellow, and its habit of visiting gardens to feed on scraps put out for it, make it one of the most endearing and best-known of British birds. You will often be able to watch the blue tit at close range, particularly in the winter, when it will be attracted to the bird table to feed on nuts.

FACT FILE

Distribution Throughout Europe except the far north of Scandinavia. Also present in north-western Africa

Size 12cm/5in

Habitat Wooded areas in parks and gardens

Nest Tree holes

Eggs 7–16, white with reddish-brown markings

Food Invertebrates, seeds and nuts

House Sparrow

Passer domesticus

A common sight on bird tables and in city parks, house sparrows have adapted to living alongside people, even to the extent of nesting under roofs in buildings. These sparrows form loose flocks, with larger numbers congregating where food is available. They spend much of their time on the ground, hopping along and ever watchful for passing predators, such as cats. It is not uncommon for them to construct nests during the winter time, which are used as communal roosts rather than for breeding. The bills of cock birds turn black at the start of the nesting period in the spring. In rural areas, house sparrows will sometimes nest in tree hollows.

The black bib of the male is a helpful spotting feature.

IDENTIFICATION

- Red-brown head; grey area on top. A black stripe runs across the eyes. Broad black bib extends over chest.
- Has a whitish area under the tail.
- The ear coverts and the entire underparts are greyish.
- Females are a duller shade of brown with a pale stripe behind each eye and a fawn bar on each wing.

FACT FILE

Distribution Occurs throughout virtually all of Europe and eastwards into Asia. Also present in both North and south-eastern Africa
Size 15cm/6in
Habitat Urban and more rural areas
Nest Buildings and tree hollows
Eggs 3–6, whitish with darker markings
Food Seeds and invertebrates, which are especially sought during the breeding season

Wren

Troglodytes troglodytes

Although this bird's tiny size makes it hard to spot, its loud song betrays its presence. Wrens are often found in areas where there is plenty of cover, such as ivy-clad walls, where they hunt for food, scurrying under the vegetation in search of spiders and similar prey. In winter, when their small size could make them vulnerable to hypothermia, wrens huddle together in roosts overnight to keep warm. The male wren establishes his territory by singing loudly from a perch. He is most vocal in March, when courtship and nest-building begin. The hen chooses one of several nests that the male constructs, lining it with feathers to form a soft base for her eggs.

The wren often cocks its tail.

IDENTIFICATION

- Reddish-brown back and wings with barring. Lighter brown underparts and a narrow eye stripe.
- Short tail, greyish on its underside.
- Bill is long and relatively narrow.
- Sexes are alike.

FACT FILE

Distribution Resident throughout Europe, apart from Scandinavia and neighbouring parts of Russia during the winter. Wrens in Europe move south in the winter. Present in North Africa
Size 10cm/4in
Habitat Overgrown gardens and woodland
Nest Ball-shaped, in any well-hidden spot
Eggs 5–6, white with reddish-brown markings
Food Mainly invertebrates

Eurasian Nuthatch

Sitta europaea

The large, strong feet and powerful claws of the Eurasian nuthatch give a hint as to the behaviour of these birds. They are adept at scampering up and down tree trunks, hunting for invertebrates, which they extract with their narrow bills. Their compact and powerful beaks also enable them to feed on nuts. First they wedge a nut into a suitable crevice in the bark, then they hammer at the shell, breaking it open so they can extract the kernel. Nuthatches also store nuts, which they can use when other food is in short supply. Their bills have another use, too – plastering over the entrance to the nesting hole in the spring. The small opening just allows the birds to squeeze in, helping to protect them from predators. Eurasian nuthatches are most likely to be encountered in areas that have broad-leafed trees, because these provide food such as acorns and hazelnuts.

▼ *This bird is fairly easy to spot because it is always moving about and has a distinctive shape: small and plump with a long head, long and narrow bill and short tail.*

The tail is short and has distinctive black stripes.

The Eurasian nuthatch has a plump body.

The narrow bill is ideal for extracting invertebrates from the bark of trees.

This is the only European bird that can walk head-first down a tree-trunk.

IDENTIFICATION

- Bluish-grey upperparts from head to tail. Black stripes on the short tail.

- A black stripe runs across the eye area.

- Cheeks and throat are white.

- Bill rather like a woodpecker's.

- Underparts vary in colour, depending on the race, from white through to a rusty shade of buff.

- Dark reddish-brown rear area.

- Sexes are alike, except that the red-brown rear is a brighter colour in the males.

BIRDWATCH

This is an easy bird to recognize as it is the only one that habitually descends trees head downwards, moving with a jerky gait. It uses its narrow bill to extract invertebrates from the bark. It also feeds on nuts and seeds, wedging the tougher items into cracks in the bark so that it can hammer them open.

FACT FILE

Distribution Found throughout most of Europe, apart from Ireland, northern England, Scotland and much of Scandinavia. Occurs in North Africa opposite the Strait of Gibraltar

Size 14cm/5.5in

Habitat Gardens and parks with mature trees

Nest In a secluded spot

Eggs 6–9, white with heavy reddish-brown speckling

Food Invertebrates and seeds

Willow Warbler

Phylloscopus trochilus

The subdued colouring of these small birds is very effective camouflage. So, despite being one of Europe's most common birds, willow warblers are quite hard to spot, especially in the wooded areas where they are often found. However, their song, which heralds their arrival in the spring, betrays their presence. In the British Isles, the willow warbler is the most numerous warbler, with a population estimated at three million pairs. It is usually resident in Europe between April and September. Its nest is well hidden in vegetation. In late summer, these birds are often seen in loose association with various tits, before heading off to their wintering grounds in Africa.

A distinctive yellow streak runs across the eyes.

The tail is long and slightly forked.

IDENTIFICATION

- Greyish-green upperparts, with a pale yellowish streak running across the eyes.
- Pale yellow throat and chest, with whitish underparts.
- The yellow plumage is much whiter in birds from more northern areas.

FACT FILE

Distribution Occurs in the summer from the British Isles right across northern Europe. Overwinters in Africa
Size 12cm/5in
Habitat Areas with plenty of trees
Nest Domed, built on the ground
Eggs 6–7, pale pink with reddish spotting
Food Small invertebrates

European Serin

Serinus serinus

Although mainly confined to relatively southerly latitudes, these serins are occasionally seen in the British Isles and have even bred successfully in southern England. It appears that serins are slowly extending their northerly distribution. Ornithological records reveal that they had spread to central Europe by 1875, and had started to colonize France within another 50 years. Serins often seek out stands of conifers, where they nest, although they also frequent citrus groves further south in their range. Young birds are quite different in appearance from adults, being predominantly brown and lacking any yellow in their plumage.

◀ *The female (top) is duller than the male (bottom).*

FACT FILE

IDENTIFICATION

- A bright yellow forehead, extending in a stripe above the eyes, circling the cheeks down on to the breast.
- Back is yellow and streaked with brown, as are the white flanks.
- Females are duller, with a pale yellow rump.

Distribution Resident in coastal areas of France south through the Iberian Peninsula to North Africa and around the northern Mediterranean area. A summer visitor elsewhere in mainland Europe
Size 12cm/5in
Habitat Parks and gardens
Nest Cup-shaped, in tree
Eggs 3–5, pale blue with darker markings
Food Seeds and some invertebrates

Chaffinch

Fringilla coelebs

The chaffinch is resident in Britain throughout the year, and in winter is joined by populations from northern and eastern Europe. They can all be seen together in groups during the winter, but in spring, when the breeding season starts, cock birds become very territorial, driving away any rivals. The male moves into dense cover and courts the female by approaching her in a lopsided crouch, followed by singing and other displays. Once lured into his territory, the female looks for a suitable nest site in a bush, hedge or small tree. Chaffinches usually prefer to feed on the ground, hopping along in search of seeds. They seek invertebrates almost exclusively for rearing their chicks.

◀ *A female (top) and male (bottom) chaffinch. The male bird's colouring is much more striking and contrasting than the female's.*

The chaffinch's beak is adapted to crush tough seed husks.

Male and female birds have the same tail colouring.

IDENTIFICATION

- Has a black band above the bill with grey over the head and neck.
- The cheeks and underparts are pinkish.
- The back is brown with two distinctive white wing bars.
- Males are less brightly coloured in winter plumage.
- Females have dull grey cheek patches and dark greyish-green upperparts. Their underparts are a buff shade of greyish white.

BIRDWATCH

The male chaffinch is one of Britain's most attractive birds. It is easily identified by its grey-blue neck and crown, pinkish brown cheeks and underparts, and chestnut back. Female chaffinches are brownish-fawn with grey-brown underparts. The British chaffinch has a purer pink breast and paler colouring than those from other parts of Europe.

FACT FILE

Distribution Resident in the British Isles and western Europe, and a summer visitor to Scandinavia and eastern Europe. Also occurs in North Africa. Resident in the west of North Africa and at the south-western tip of Africa

Size 16cm/6in

Habitat Woodland in parks and gardens

Nest Cup-shaped, in a tree fork

Eggs 4–5, light brown or blue with dark, often smudgy markings

Food Seeds and some invertebrates

European Goldfinch

Carduelis carduelis

▼ *The male (bottom) has totally different facial colouring to the female (top).*

Narrow bills let these birds prise kernels out of seeds, and in winter they often feed on thistle heads and teasel. Goldfinches are very agile, capable of clinging to narrow stems when feeding. Social by nature, they gather in small flocks where food is plentiful, although they are shy when feeding on the ground. They have a loud, attractive, twittering song and prefer to build nests in tree-forks rather than hiding them in a hedge.

IDENTIFICATION

- Bright red face. Black area on the crown. White extends around the throat, and a brown necklace separates it from the paler underparts. Brown back and flanks.
- Bill is narrow and pointed.
- Black wings with white spotting and yellow bars. Tail is black with white markings.
- Females have duller coloration.

FACT FILE

Distribution Occurs throughout much of the British Isles and mainland Europe, including Denmark but confined to the extreme south of Scandinavia. Also present in North Africa

Size 13cm/5in

Habitat Woodland and more open areas

Nest Cup-shaped, made of vegetation

Eggs 5–6, bluish white with darker markings

Food Seeds and invertebrates

European Greenfinch

Carduelis chloris

The greenfinch has a stout conical bill for cracking seeds.

Greenfinches have stout bills that allow them to crack open seed casings to reach the edible kernels inside. These birds are most likely to be seen where there are trees and bushes to provide cover for nesting. In the winter, the European greenfinch is a frequent visitor to the garden, where it will take peanuts from a bird feeder as well as foraging for invertebrates. Groups of greenfinches may also be sighted in open areas of countryside, such as farmland, where they search for weed seeds and grains that have been dropped during harvesting. Pairs often nest two or three times a year and invertebrates are consumed in larger quantities when there are chicks in the nest.

IDENTIFICATION

- Greenish head, with greyer areas on the sides of the face and wings. Quite large, conical bill.
- Yellowish-green breast, with yellow evident on flight feathers.
- Female is duller, with greyer tone overall, brownish mantle and less yellow on the wings.

FACT FILE

Distribution Throughout Europe and North Africa apart from the far north of Scandinavia

Size 16cm/6in

Habitat Edges of woodland and more open areas

Nest Bulky, cup-shaped

Eggs 4–6, whitish to pale blue with darker markings

Food Largely seeds and some invertebrates

GLOSSARY

Adapt To change over many generations in order to survive better in a particular environment.
Anatomy How the body of a bird is constructed.
Anvil A rock or other hard object against which some species batter prey such as snails, in order to break the shell.
Aquatic Living in water.
Camouflage The colour and markings that help hide a bird in its surroundings.
Carrion The rotting flesh of a dead animal.
Clutch The number of eggs in a bird's nest.
Colony A large group of the same species all living together.
Coniferous Cone-bearing trees such as pines and firs, that usually have needles rather than leaves.
Contour feathers The smaller feathers that cover the head and body of a bird.
Cover Bushes and undergrowth in which a bird can hide away from predators.
Coverts Feathers covering the wings and also found at the base of the tail.
Courtship display The special way in which a male behaves in order to attract a female.
Crepuscular A bird that becomes active at dusk.
Crown The top of a bird's head.
Deciduous Trees that shed their leaves in winter.
Dormant Sleeping or hibernating during cold weather, when supplies of food are scarce.

Down The small, soft feathers close to the bird's body that conserve heat.
Eclipse plumage The plumage that some species have outside the breeding season.
Feral Domesticated or human-introduced creatures that have escaped and established wild populations in areas where they were not originally native.
Flank The side of a bird from the chest to the legs.
Fledge To bring up a young bird until it is ready to fly.
Flush To disturb a bird and cause it to fly off.
Fossil The remains of a bird, plant or animal turned to stone.
Habitat The natural home of a bird species.
Hawk To hunt while flying in the air (on the wing).
Host species A bird that has either the egg or the young of another bird (a cuckoo, for example) in its nest.
Hypothermia Dangerously low body temperature caused by exposure to cold weather.
Incubate To sit on eggs in order to hatch them.
Insectivorous Eating insects.
Invertebrate An animal without a backbone.
Iridescence Glittering colours on the feathers.
Migrant A bird that undertakes regular migrations.
Migration Moving from one place to another, usually for breeding purposes.
Mimicry When a bird behaves like another species.
Moult To lose feathers. When birds moult, one set of feathers is replaced by another.
Nestling A young bird that is still in the nest.
Nocturnal Hunting and feeding at night.
Opportunistic feeder A bird that eats whatever is available, including carrion.

Overwinter To spend the winter in a particular place.
Parasitic A bird that takes advantage of another, such as a cuckoo laying its eggs in another bird's nest.
Pesticide Chemical sprayed on to crops in fields to kill insects and other pests.
Plumage Feathers.
Predator An animal or bird that preys on (hunts) another.
Preen To clean and neatly arrange the feathers.
Quarry A hunted animal (prey).
Range The area in which a species lives.
Regurgitate To bring back up after swallowing.
Road kill Animals killed by cars on the road.
Rufous Reddish in colour.
Rump The rear part of a typical bird's body.
Scavenge To search for food on rubbish tips.
Social Living in a group.
Species A group of birds with similar characteristics such as body shape.
Specialized hunter A bird that obtains its food in one particular way, such as a kingfisher.
Taiga A marshy area of pine forest in the far north of Europe, south of the tundra.
Tarsal The area at or below the ankle in birds.
Territory An area that a bird treats as its own.
Thermal A current of rising hot air.
Tundra Arctic region with permanently frozen subsoil and very little vegetation.

INDEX